# Grandmother Moon Wonders

Matthilda May Brown

**BALBOA.**
PRESS

A DIVISION OF HAY HOUSE

Balboa Press books may be ordered through booksellers or by contacting:

Balboa Press
A Division of Hay House
1663 Liberty Drive
Bloomington, IN 47403
www.balboapress.com.au
1 (877) 407-4847

Print information available on the last page.

ISBN: 978-1-5043-1536-4 (sc)
ISBN: 978-1-5043-1537-1 (e)

Balboa Press rev. date: 11/05/2018

# Contents

*Stories to set you thinking*

THE SHADOW
POETIC JUSTICE
OLD SALTY
THE MESSAGE STICK
TWELVE STEPS
DAM DEATH
SIRENS OF KARMA
NO GRATITUDE IN APRIL
THE LEGEND OF THE EAGLE MEDICINE
VERMILLION - THE SWEET EAR AFTER
CAESAR'S QUIETUS
THE OMEGA CHRONICLES
TRAIN RIDE TO NANPULGUDGERI

Matthilda May Brown

*This collection of stories travels forward into the future and way back into the past. The characters may be Irish or Indian or Atlantean, Native American, African, New Zealand or Australian. They might remind you of your neighbour, your friend or a family member.*

*You might even find a part of yourself in some of them.*

*All of my stories, except the first, experience death in some way.*

*This is not to be morbid, but to reveal the magic in endings. From endings come new beginnings - if we let them.*

*The last story shows the wonder of 'letting go' in readiness to be emptied.*

*Only when we are empty can we be filled.*

*When we accept that we don't create because we are afraid of failing...*

*...then we can empty out our preconceived notions of success and...*

*embrace our shadow.....*

*GM*

# THE SHADOW

This thing I have, gifted to me from Ireland, has been a delicious joy and a nightmarish terror. It, this thing, took me into people's hearts and homes and dreams - and not only human people. Tree and plant families; rock Elders; animal parents and infants; bees and birds and every flighted and crawling thing as well. What a wonder is this thing!

The part of the gift, the one that thrilled me the most, was the part that could transform all these conversations and places and happenings into wondrous words on paper. Words that could draw a gasp, leak an eye, ponder a brain or gurgle a throat. Words that danced like flames, flowed like lava and sighed like my old mother.

All life was spoken for and understood by my words.

Then one dull, wet day in old Sydney town my gift was stolen. Not that I knew of course. It wasn't like losing one's keys or even a husband. Those would have been obvious. That morning, the only clue was the currawong that had a leer in its eye. I know, I know bird eyes don't leer, but this bird definitely did. All day I searched for my gift. Well actually it was only half the gift that was missing – the wondrous word part. Traipsing around in torrents of rain I questioned every green or breathing thing and even a sculpture of mighty Gilgamesh. All of which had much to say of course, but I felt that the loss of wondrous words was a dark embarrassment for us all.

Have you ever tried to pull a stuck calf out of its poor wailing mother? Or watch a callous fisherman twist and tug a rusty hook from a fish's wee mouth while its eyes bulged in terror? Or perhaps you've pressed your mouth over an unconscious homeless person? Kneeling in the filthy gutter where he fell, ignoring his smell and germs willing him to breathe again?

Well this is how I searched for my gift. Using all my strength to save the 'calf', all of my fury at my own heartlessness and all of my resolve to do what had to be done.

Then I slipped and fell in the gutter.

Not beside a derelict, but under a monolithic fig tree. Naturally I told it how magnificent it was, while I sat sodden and entranced by its roots. The entire landscape under the trees was another dimension; or rather like the macro world reduced in size. The roots rose sublimely from the soil like the Great Dividing Range snaking down the east coast. Little ant persons, protected by the gargantuan fig-umbrella climbed those mountains – tiny packs on their wee backs. Other fig roots were like pterodactyl claws or komodo dragons. It was all truly entrancing.

Ah! but I digress.

Essentially the trees said that I needed to go to my roots. Instead I slopped my way to a tasteless dinner and then to bed. Oh I tried the wondrous words on a page thing first, but only withered, weary words appeared. Frustrated as that poor cow I was. So I gave myself to sleep, traipsing through the astral worlds instead, hoping for an answer.

A shadowy figure rose up from the path in front of me.

"I believe I have something of yours m'dear!" it gloated.

Fear gripped my throat with cold, cutting fingers. I wanted to get back to my body, but in one single thump of my heart, I knew that I wanted my gift more.

"Give it back!" I screamed.

"Come and get it," the Shadow smirked.

I lunged then, sure I'd bring it to heel, wrest my gift from him. Instead he stepped sideways and I hurtled into space – falling, falling, tumbling and crumbling.

"You can only have it when you get to the bottom," the Shadow laughed after me.

*When you get to the bottom... to the bottom... the bottom...* echoed the voice.

"To the bottom of what!" I yelled and woke m'silly self up.

Begorrah it was morning!

Leer, the currawong, fixed me with one yellow eye and said, "When you get to the bottom of your fear of *failing*, that's what!"

I'll be calling that bird the Shadow from now on.

*Shadows have long held a sense of the hidden, the mysterious and sometimes the macabre.*

*Our shadow-selves are believed to be what is hidden from us; those aspects of character that hold the keys to freedom, which we can't see...so I wondered...*

*If our fears, and our phobias hide in the shadows of our projected personalities, then what is required to expose them?*

*And if they are exposed, what then? Freedom?*

*And what is freedom? Should we fear it or embrace it? Freedom comes at a price.*
*Perhaps it is better to stay in the shadows.*

*I think not.*
*You decide........*

GM

# POETIC JUSTICE

Mildred eats far better than most elderly people and would be obese, but guilt can gnaw away at one's glucose like rats eating through a pantry. She always found an excuse when it came to nourishing anything other than herself. The years have shrunk and bent her but Mildred still intimidates. Cruelty and hostility can bend a person so out of shape they stay that way and reputable living doesn't disguise her nature as easily as she thinks. When Mildred arrives at Bowls, other women stiffen and whisper 'bigoted cow' and 'hateful bitch', while they clutch teacups with gnarly knuckles and chew their antacids.

Mildred Murphy's sense of smell, like her hearing, is more diminished than her wrath. She couldn't smell a rotten egg if she sat on it, but she could smell a stalker as if he were right up her bulbous nose. Mildred collected the mail from her rusty letterbox and as though it were hurt by her touch, the box squealed as she wrestled the lid open. Another plain envelope. Another threat scrawled on a white A4 sheet.

"I know who you are," she said aloud as she stashed the letter in a cupboard in the garage, "and you'll be sorry." Mildred sang the word 'sorry' in a mischievous child-like voice, then with a grunt she slammed the garage door and locked it; rolled her thin lips together to check her lipstick; patted her white poodle-permed hair; straightened her polyester dress and walked with purpose to the bus stop.

Meanwhile and miles away, her daughter Lilli began a day she would never forget.

***

Just short of being obsessive/compulsive, Lilly was a practising Psychologist. She preferred to call herself 'Life Coach' as she knew she epitomised a wounded healer. Lilly was meticulous in her physical, mental and emotional habits. Each one dominated her existence and every moment was committed to order; a schedule she followed as rigorously as a soldier in camp. This was her sanctuary.

She now paused beside the trill of the ringing phone, jiggled her skewed neck and silently chanted a mantra she had developed - *prepare for the known, but embrace the unexpected*. With the cold plastic against her ear, she put a smile into her voice before speaking. "Good morning. This is Lilly. How can I help?"

A woman's voice told her 'sorry wrong number' and she delighted in the reprieve. Lilly had a refined level-headedness that she had forged from adversity. Despite that, for over forty years she had secretly craved a hero; someone who would go into battle for her; fight for her honour; demand retribution for her injustices and protect her. While waiting for this hero, she believed that discipline led to freedom and that everything had a consequence, so her ordered mind was able to stretch into the future and have a plan ready for all consequences. Until this day.

When the doorbell rang, she smiled one of her brilliant grins at a skinny young man through the wire.

"Yes?"

"I'm from the RTA, just letting you know we're re-surfacing your street."

"Does that mean I can't drive on it?" Already Lilly's mind leapt to plan 'B' just in case.

"Only for about three hours all up."

"Thanks so much. Have fun." Lilly smiled at the man and went straight to the pantry. Planning needed fuel, but she shocked herself when she shovelled liquorice bullets into her mouth and swallowed them barely chewed. Yet she decided that the sweet juice of liquorice and melting chocolate sliding down her throat was compensation for blackening her teeth. Nevertheless, discipline dictated immediate teeth cleaning. She smiled as she remembered telling her children, 'only clean the ones you want to keep.'

In the mirror over the basin she glimpsed him. Elderly, bald and beefy with pasty skin, he moved passed her *ensuite* door unaware he'd been spotted. Lilly's mind – her disciplined, ordered mind – seemed to her, to be chaotically out of control. *I'll keep pretending to clean my teeth. If he comes near me I'll stick him in the eye with my toothbrush.* Plan 'A' was now operational and she tried to recall some of her karate moves from thirty years ago. Lilly decided the testicle crushing ones would probably be the best choice, but then she noticed the flaccid muscles hanging on her twiggy arms and knew that combat would end badly.

At the other end of the street the bitumen truck was starting a slow groan. The young man who rang Lilly's doorbell and two others were blowing dust from the roadway in front of it. The noise of the blowers was bizarre and forced Lilly to opt for plan 'B' as no one would hear her screams if plan 'A' went badly. Lilly held the retch in her mouth and despite her terror, scolded herself for not chewing the bullets better. Only her discipline saved her from vomiting up the contents of her stomach. She had a long history of controlling her feelings, which began almost from babyhood. Every abused child must learn different survival techniques and Lilly believed her competent persona had served her well and offered security to her children. Plan 'B' demanded the 'wise, compassionate counsellor' approach. Lilly's heart was thumping painfully against her sternum as she left the *ensuite*, scanning the bedroom with enormous eyes. Empty. She slipped into the hallway, looking this way and that. Empty. Lilly walked tentatively toward the family room, checking behind her with neck swivelling as fast as a broken battery-toy.

"You don't remember me, I suppose." His rich gravy voice didn't match his appearance. Lilly jumped in spite of her commitment to calmness and then saw that the old man's face was disfigured with an horrific burn scar.

'Humour him Lilly' she silently coached herself.

"I believe I do, as a matter of fact." She coughed softly as tiny needles pricked her throat. "I just can't remember your name, I'm sorry. Menopause is a bitch y'know!"

"You're a clever girl. Menopause? You? Are you really that old?" The resonance of his voice mesmerised Lilly. He swayed a little suddenly seeming ill.

"I guess you must be," he said breathing the words out.

"Please sit down. Are you OK?" Lilly couldn't help herself, despite the danger. Plan 'B' told her that it would be hard for him to jump her if he was sitting and she would also have a head start if she decided to run for it. The man began to edge stubby fingers toward his inside coat pocket and Lilly froze. She couldn't outrun a bullet. Plan 'C' was needed. But what if it was a knife instead? The sound of her breath was like surf pounding in her ears and her palms were slick with sweat. The doorbell's ding-dong made them both start and their eyes locked. The old man shrugged, "You may as well get that. Go on. I'm not going anywhere."

Lilly backed away from him into the hallway trying to configure plan 'C', then opened the door a crack. Sticking through the grid of the screen door was a note canvassing for window cleaning, but the porch was otherwise empty. The bitumen truck groaned closer, yet was still not in sight. Lilly inched back to the family room unable to reckon why she didn't make a run for freedom. A menopausal heat turned her skin red and sweat bled from every pore.

The room was empty but through the glass door she saw him in the back yard. Plan 'C' wasn't going too well.

"Nice little garden you've got here," the man called above the truck noise. "I grow my own vegies too. Reckon it's in the blood."

Despite the psychobabble in her brain that issued alarm warnings, Lilly immediately warmed to him. The man held a sheet of paper in his hand and waved it at her.

"Come here, I've got something to read to you." He patted the grass beside him in the shade.

"What say I put the kettle on and get some cake?" Lilly quipped as though they were about to have a picnic. All her plans were abandoned as she decided 'a man who grows his own vegies can't be all bad? Can he?'

A catch of crows settled on the TV aerial and as if observing her folly cried loudly, 'a-a-a-a-r-r-k, f-u-u-u-u-k-k!'

"That'd great. Black tea thanks Lilly," the old man said."

Lilly panicked. *'Oh! Shit, he knows my name.'*

With the tea tray between them she sat and managed a trembling smile as she poured.

"So aren't you going to tell me your name?"

He shook his head. "Not yet." The scars stretched cruelly at each turn of his head. He took spectacles from his shirt pocket and began reading from the paper he held.

*"Party Line, by Lillian Ceili Murphy.*

*You laugh like a drunken man Mummy.*
*Red lipstick flashing*

*white teeth through nicotine stain.*
*Do you fancy you're a film star?*

*Flinging your good body onto that man.*

*Where's my Daddy? Not at this party.*
*Come 'ere and dance Lady Jane,*
    *bleeding mouth mother yells.*
*I gyrate my eight-year-old bones.*
*She whispers in his ear -*
*George, the toy train driver from the Carnival.*

*Climb aboard Beautiful, he'd winked at me.*
*I loved him in that moment.*
*Hated them both now. Run out. Run and run.*
*Where's the little buggar going she yells,*

*spilling whisky on him.*

*He leers. Now you'll have to lick it off.*
    *I run so hard around and around*
    *into other kids playing in the night*
    *into a clothesline, shrubs and dark sheds.*

*Why isn't my Daddy here?*

*Who are you? You shouldn't be out here.*
*Boy's soft blanket voice wraps around me*
*Blocks my ears to shrieking mothers.*
*Well you are, I say.*

*Think a girl should be afraid of the dark?*

*Boy opens the door of the old FJ.*
*Climb aboard Beautiful.*

*He winks at me*
*you shouldn't be afraid of anything.*

*That's what they all said."*

The old man's fingers clenched the paper like meat hooks into flesh. Tremulously he pocketed the poem again. Lilly felt a vein in her forehead pulse demandingly.

"Why are you reading me this poem?"

"You *are* Lillian Ceili Murphy aren't you? That's not a common name?" He tried to sound nonchalant, but Lilly could taste the bitterness in his words. The 'wise, compassionate counsellor' of plan 'B' was given full throttle.

"You seem angry at this Lillian Murphy. Would you be comfortable telling me why?"

Without warning the man grabbed Lilly's shoulder and she saw how scarred and tortured his arm and hand were. He let her go as quickly as he pounced.

"I'm not angry with her – Geezus girl, can we stop playing games – you are Lillian Murphy aren't you?"

"I'll tell you who I am, but you have to tell me who you are first." Lilly's compassion was genuine and out-ranked her fear. She reached for his podgy hand and pressed it lightly. Without warning, the old man's ample chest began quivering and tears dripped onto his collar. The water made his scars smooth and slimy-looking.

"I'm Shaun Murphy, your father, Lilly. I've been lookin' for you for over forty years." Emotion accentuated the Irish lilt in his voice.

"Daddy? Oh! Daddy." Incredulously, Lilly allowed a dam of suppressed emotions to burst down her face and she wept for them both, but mostly she cried because her hero had finally found her. The maiden was released from the tower. Uneasy, awkward silences were punctuated then with father and daughter blurting questions in perfect synchronicity. "What happened to you after the fire?" Then laughing together as people do and saying also in unison, "it's such a long story" and "I don't know where to start."

They were unaware of the shadowy figure hiding in the garage, two metres from where they sat. Shaun told Lilly that he had read her published memoir and how the guilt of not protecting her from her mother consumed his hours.

"This poem," he patted his shirt pocket, "lit a fire in my belly so fierce, that I decided to confront your mother."

"You know where she is?"

"Oh! Yes indeed I do. I live only a street away from the old bag. We pass each other sometimes, but she doesn't recognise me – head up her own bum as always! Or maybe it's the scars. Or this?" Shaun added derisively, patting his substantial belly.

"Daddy, what do you mean 'confront' her? Perhaps we should leave sleeping dogs lie?"

Shaun lay back on the grass and covered his face with his hands.

"Go and get a copy of your book, there's a good girl."

Lilly sensed a presence as she passed the back door to the garage, but her inner turmoil overrode it and she returned with her memoir. Shaun sat up abruptly, grabbed the book and found what he was looking for. Before he started reading Lilly's own words to her he hissed, "this is one mongrel dog who I'm *not* going to let lie Lilly!"

Shaun read through a constricted throat, making each word darker and dirtier, while an interloper in the garage was silently, methodically collecting any combustible material to be found and piling it against the house wall.

*"I was still in my dressing gown when the doorbell rang that morning. With the baby on a hip I opened the door to George. He looked agitated and his tie was crooked.*

*I put the baby in her cot and got her interested in some toys then fled to the bathroom. I madly brushed my teeth then combed my hair as George came up behind me. He pressed into me and the mirror showed his clenched jaw, emotionally controlled and rigid as my mother. In the* same second that I sensed his anger he attacked like a tomcat killing its innocent progeny.

"You bitch, I thought you were too good to be true!" he snarled. I helplessly did nothing, while he struck me in a perfect monotone. His words beating like a drum to the metronome of his hand. Mildred my mother, and George had merged . "You little bitch" – strike – "I'll give it to you" – strike – "I told you" –strike – "you'll do as I say" – strike – strike – strike. I lost consciousness. Then regained it as I hit the mattress. George was tearing his trousers off. Then he was on me, pinning my arms to the bed, fingers bruising to the bone, forcing himself into me. His anger was volcanic. This was an eruption that no one could outrun. His fiery lava erupted inside my vagina while one gorilla-hand capped my head and crushed neck vertebrae. The other hand covered my screaming mouth."

Unconsciously Lilly's hands went to her skewed neck and as another wave of heat hit her body she laid back on the grass. In that moment she realised that Fate would always laugh at her feeble attempts to control her destiny.

"F-u-u-c-c-k-k." Lilly chorused with the crows with a sardonic grin.

She was astounded at her father's fierce reaction to her history and was relieved that the bitumen truck was now outside her house, making a fearful noise.

"George is as old as you by now and maybe even dead, Daddy. Let it go. What's done is done. Forget about Mum too. You and I can have a new beginning," she yelled.

Then a woman's raspy voice, shouting to be heard over the truck, astounded them both.

"Yeah! That's right; forget about me. No-one cares about Mildred!" She held up a petrol tin, shaking it like a fist. I'll give you something to remember me by!" Mildred turned and ran back into the garage. Lilly and Shaun scrambled after her, screaming for her to stop.

In the gloom of the garage, flames were licking up the house wall and Mildred cackled like a ghoul at an execution. Lilly pressed the remote control and the front roller-door ground open. The blast of fresh air intensified the fire. Flames leapt from the pile of rubbish and stretched scorching fingers out to the old woman. She shrieked and backed away, then as surely as if she'd been pushed, she tripped and fell like a shop dummy off a truck. In horror they watched as she rolled down the steep driveway straight under the heaving machinery pouring hot tar onto the road.

***

Mildred was dead. The owner of her rented cottage cleared her ratty belongings with one fell swoop. The 'letter' cupboard in the web-infested garage ended up in his truck with all of Mildred's memories. Shaun had walked his dog passed Mildred's cottage every day, and he'd watched her stashing his 'revenge' letters into that old cupboard, certain she hadn't recognised him.

Now as a light rain fell, Shaun watched as the garbage was carted off to the Council Tip. He drove his little Toyota behind the truck and waited until its contents were dumped on the mud. The rain, heavier now, didn't stop his foraging. With trembling hands, he prised open the old cupboard and took out a shoebox. Inside was a stack of letters. The first one was illegible, but undeterred he smoothed out the next and read in his own hand writing; *"You old bitch! I'm going to get you if I have to wait a hundred years. You'll pay for what you've done to Lilly and me and no-one will ever guess who did it!"*

The rain got heavier. Shaun struck match after damp match to ignite the paper without success. His heart began banging into his ribs and electrifying pain spread across his chest and tore down his arm. Unable to stand upright Shaun fell to his knees, dropping the box amid the garbage. He watched the death letters spill across the mud like fluttering white dinner napkins on the Grim Reaper's table.

*"I wish I'd been a better husband Mildred..."*

*Writing can be a useful way to reveal our shadow...
poems, incidences, happenings that bring those
shadows*
    *out of the darkness*
        *into the light.*

*Writing can also reveal the depth
of our wisdom.*
    *I wondered if it might even be*

*the well-considered conclusion*
        *of our life's journey.*

*GM*

## OLD SALTY

Most of the residents in the Banksia retirement home were napping after lunch. Mavis Jamieson was the exception. She mumbled softly to her self as she wrote.

"One must always keep a journal if one has an ounce of intelligence. My journals, in which I conscientiously write, have faithfully recorded my deepest feelings, profound insights and most exhilarating experiences – all of which have been a rich source of novels for over sixty years. My hand does rather shake somewhat as I write these days."

*It is one of life's travesties that an inner life can be so vibrant, while one's outer appearance becomes fossilized.*

"Journals for the ignorant though, are like 'Grange Hermitage' to tee-totallers and this new nurse is as boring as a brick. Now where was I? Oh yes my fossilized self…"

*Skin once so firm, clear and resilient, now flaps like drying seaweed on a ship's hull. The hull of this old ship once stood proudly erect, her mighty mast heralding a feisty battle. Now broken and damaged by high seas and the winds of life, I'm left barely afloat in this ship's graveyard.*

"I must say, I've never referred to the other residents or myself as ships before. You see? A journal can produce wonderfully interesting ways of seeing life.

Ellen, I think the nurse's name is Ellen or Helen, something like that. Stupid girl sees nothing – head stuck firmly up her own t-shirt. Yesterday she looked at my deciduous ginkgo trees; the ones I'd grown in pots from seed; each a single leafless twig now because it is winter."

"I'll put those ugly dead things in the rubbish for you dear," she said.

"Over my dead body dearie!" I said. "Leafless doesn't mean lifeless!"

"I wrote a haiku-like piece in my journal then.

> *Potted twigs seeming dead and done*
> *Yet pointing fingers to the coming sun.*

She didn't get it – simply couldn't comprehend it. Does she think I don't have any sap in my veins either?"

***

The nurse asked Mavis Jamieson if she would like to show the doctor her journal. The old lady squinted as if processing the question then sniffed, sucking in her nostrils and said only if he drank Grange Hermitage.

The psychiatrist made a note on Mildred's patient records and whispered that there didn't seem to be any improvement. He was busy and might come back later.

Mildred opened her journal and wrote a poignant children's story then, about a clever old ship that once had sailed the seven seas and was now in a ship's graveyard. Everyone thought the ship, called 'The Wonder' was damaged, deaf and dumb, but really she had a fighting spirit and heard every word that was said about her.

'The Wonder' was planning a big adventure.

When next the salty wind stirred her ragged sails, she would sail off toward the farthest horizon abandoning everyone, who would then gasp, "Oh my god, we had no idea." And they didn't. Not one single idea.

Floating on the seawater in the wake left behind by 'The Wonder' would be nothing more than millions and millions and millions of words.

*It's been said that if wishes were fishes we'd all be casting nets in the sea;*
*so I wondered ...*
*if feathers were fantasies,*
*would we be able to fly if only we could dream enough?*
*What if leaves were lovers - green, red and brown -*
*would new ones appear each springtime*
*and old loves change and die every autumn?*

*Would there always be loves that endured until fire turned them to ash or wind ripped them from us?*

*If pebbles were poetry would we be so eager to skim them across water until they sank from sight*

*or kick them mindlessly or in frustration along a path?*

*If twigs were tales that fell from trees, would we gather them like treasures or crush them underfoot?*

*If sticks were stories, would we be so keen to burn them in fires?*

*And if a stick could tell a magical story how would it be told?*

*This is how...*

*GM*

# THE MESSAGE STICK

Ningrapo's grandfather was dead. The tribe collected wood for his funeral pyre and the red talcum earth was silky soft under their measured steps. Grandfather's spirit moved among them, lifting curly black hair from sweaty necks and blowing softly on tear-drenched cheeks. His body, painted for the journey beyond the rainbow, lay high on the litter. He had one eye open to make sure they did a good job. The tribe placed their sticks with sad reverence to their great chief, until they were satisfied that the wood would be enough to burn for more than a day. From sunset to sunset the pyre must burn, to light Grandfather's path.

His spirit whispered in Ningrapo's ear.

*"Listen my boy, listen well."*

Ningrapo's mother brought a glowing stick from the cooking fire and prodded dry leaves to ignite. Soon the pyre roared and crackled. Flames reached up to take Grandfather's body and his spirit cried out to the young man before he began his journey.

*"Ningrapo! Listen! You must answer this question and change the thinking of the world!"*

Everyone was crying; some wailing like wind in the desert, but all transfixed by the flames. The others did not hear Grandfather's words. Why did his spirit call to his grandson? Ningrapo listened carefully anyway.

*"Ningrapo! Does the wood need the flame? Without it the fire is useless. But with it, the wood is destroyed."*

The young man so loved his grandfather that he felt the words like grass feels sunshine, and the warmth of that light roused his mind and stirred his chest.

*"Does a body need a soul? Without it the body is useless. But with it...?" The answer to this is your quest Ningrapo. Make your ancestors proud!"*

The heat from the fire forced them all back. Ningrapo was confused. What did Grandfather mean? The tribe sang sad, pitiful songs as they slowly walked back to camp. They clapped their hands and played their drums. The resonance of drumsticks on deerskin throbbed in Ningrapo's blood as he watched the moon rise hesitantly in the darkening sky.

*"Change the thinking of the world,"* whispered on the wind and stirred Ningrapo's heart. Gathering rugs from his lodge he walked into the desert to sleep. Tonight, perhaps his spirit would meet with Grandfather's and he would explain what must be done. The cold, helped in by Ningrapo's sorrow, settled quickly into his bones. He made a small fire to keep wild dogs away then wrapped himself in the fur skin rugs. He thanked the jaguar and wolf for giving him their coats and offered prayers for their journeys too, then prepared for a journey of his own to the otherworld.

Ningrapo dropped into deep sleep like a dead bird from the sky, and began to dream a thousand dreams. For each dream a feather floated down and clung to him. Soon he seemed like a sleeping eagle, then Spirit Wind tickled the feathers until Ningrapo stretched giant wings and began to fly. He flew away from his tribe, from his family, from Mother and Father and from the land of his people. For many years he'd had fantasies about such adventures; fantasies of freedom and escape from rules and regulations imposed by others; now at last his fantasies had become feathers that gave him wings to fly. But he was not yet free.

Grandfather's spirit watched over Ningrapo's sleeping body, waiting for his return. Many times Ningrapo yelled in his sleep "get away from me!" or "I'll punish you for that!" and his body jerked and twitched as he wrestled demons from the otherworld. Next to his body a sleek white feather lifted gently and settled again with each thrashing move.

Love and lust fought like warriors in Ningrapo's dreaming and as in all battles, there was wounding. His wounds were deep and painful – stabs to the heart; slaps to the ego; cuts in the mind – which left bitterness in his soul. He secretly longed for the evergreen forests of his people, but in this realm of mystery, leaves truly were lovers, so Ningrapo, wandered this strange land and came to believe that one love must die, so another can live. He didn't know that this was a lie, so with fire and wind he stripped the evergreen leaves from his family tree. Surely now he would be free?

Ningrapo's mother had once told him, "We are like pebbles thrown into still water, my son. Everyone makes a ripple that changes the water. Be careful how you throw your pebbles. You can create gentle circles of beauty or make destructive splashes that erode the banks."

But in this dreaming, Ningrapo had torn off the leaves of enduring love and forgot everything he was taught by the elders. He forgot also, that pebbles are poetry and cast them angrily and without ceremony, into the waters of Life. This is what broken hearts do. They forget that real love cannot be lost or traded.

Sometimes he kicked a pebble along the road of this Dream Life. Sometimes it was a carefree, happy kick during times when he expected nothing and fully lost himself in the poetry of the moment. At other times Ningrapo kicked pebbles so hard in anger that the echoes were felt all the way to where Grandfather sat waiting his return.

*"The pebbles are your Soul's song Ningrapo,"* Grandfather whispered. *"Don't kick them away. Pick them up and put them in your pocket, so one day you can take them out and tell your story with them."*

Ningrapo's head was full of tales. For every twig that fell from a tree, someone had a tale to tell him. He was sick of listening to people's tales – tales of wondrous love; tales of learning; tales of suffering; tales that blurted from pleading faces and tales that spurted from bleeding hearts. He stomped on and crushed all the twiggy-tales because he could only see his own despair.

*"Collect all the twigs Ningrapo. One day you will use them to kindle your own fire. You will burn either way – better it be with compassion than with ignorance."*

Grandfather watched over Ningrapo's journey and hoped that he'd been heard. *"Have you forgotten your quest my boy? Does the body need a Soul? Without it, the body is useless – yes. Now find out what it is to be <u>with</u> it!"*

In the Otherworld, Ningrapo's Soul was lost. He moved in that world like a shadow with no substance. And no freedom. His feathers had long disappeared; erased along with his fantasies. All his leaves were dead or dying, along with his loves. He had cast his pebbles with so much bitterness, that the pool of his mind was turbulent and muddy. Ningrapo was unable to see that every twig told a tale of a Soul and should be respected. The greatest shame was that he couldn't answer Grandfather's question.

*\*\*\**

The white feather, blown by Grandfather's breath, tickled his face and he squinted his eyes in the orange glare of a setting sun. Ningrapo had been asleep for almost two days, when he woke, yet it seemed to him like a thousand moons. He drank the water in his skin flask and then examined his body, as though seeing it for the first time. He lifted his hands up to his eyes in wonder. Lines inscribed on his palms eons ago were like a map asking to be followed.

*"Your destiny lays here Ningrapo. In each hand is a treasure map. Follow the signs."*

"Grandfather, what must I do? I fear I have failed you. What is it to be with a Soul?" Ningrapo waited for his grandfather's reply, but all he heard was wind raking leaves and birds calling to their own. Ningrapo was hungry in his belly, yet there was a greater hunger in his Soul - to follow the map. He looked again at his hands; stretched them open wide and closed them into a fist and opened again, and still the lines on his palms begged to be followed.

Ningrapo walked pensively to his grandfather's funeral pyre, now a pile of ashes with a few bones visible. The sun was setting but Ningrapo knew he wasn't ready to go back to his village. He wasn't ready because he didn't know how to *'change the thinking of the world'*. Perhaps Grandfather might tell him how he, a young warrior, might ever be able to do that. He decided to build a fire and stay awhile, so looking for unburnt timber he walked around the grey ashes that were animated by the breeze.

There was one stick, long and smooth and fat, so Ningrapo reached for it, brushing the cold ashes away. Next to the stick Grandfather's skull appeared. Ningrapo sucked in his breath and jumped back, angry with himself for showing fear. Grandfather's spirit gently soothed him and calmed his pounding heart.

*"The feathers, pebbles, twigs and sticks of your life have taken you on a journey that you found wanting Ningrapo. From your desperation will come inspiration! Take this stick in your hands and do what must be done, my boy!"*

In that moment Ningrapo knew what he must do. The same

as he knew to breathe and in the breathing he would find a space so empty of longing that it fills the universe with itself. Resonating and rebounding through the galaxies, that home-space danced in starlight, played music of angels and painted rainbows of throbbing colours. It whispered its own name, and then like nesting birds settled in his heart.

*** 

The old lady fingered the stick in her hands as though feeling silken cloth...gently and with reverence for its beauty. Her bones hurt to sit on the earth, so she sat hunched forward on a log at the campfire. Grandmother Sinequan was so old that the tribe believed she walked in two worlds and that was how she could live twice as long as the rest of them. Sinequan was blind so she was able to see things that others who have eyes, could not.

"Tonight I will tell you the story of one Ningrapo, who lived many moons ago," she said. "He carved this message stick for us and for those who come after us. This is his story." She began reading his carving through gnarly fingers.

*'I, Ningrapo have been told from beyond the rainbow to change the thinking of the world, so listen carefully. Every thing of the earth is sacred and come as gifts to remind us who we are. But we humans are judgemental, temperamental and sentimental. We forget that we come from the four elements of creation - Fire, Earth, Water and Air. All elements are to be honoured and absorbed into our being. You must look at what elements you have grown, what you have overgrown or what you have neglected. Is it passion, urge and courage of Fire? Is it Earth that gives you strength with a desire to protect and nurture? Perhaps it is Air for quick thinking, reasoning and inspiration or Water's gift of empathy, compassion and intuition?'*

Sinequan breathed deeply, waiting for the words to make impact on the tribe, before continuing.

*'A single leaf cannot survive without the tree and so it is with us.*

*Like a single leaf you will be blown wherever Wind wants and however ferocious the blast. Anchor yourself to the tree of your Soul-family with love and understanding. Just as a bird cannot fly without feathers, so we cannot be all that we can be without proper dreaming. For every dream we have, a bird loses a feather. Be careful what you dream. Your dreams can lead you to fly, so be clear where it is you want to be. Not every dream leads you to freedom. A sacred web connects us to all of life. The web feels if even one single strand is being touched. Therefore you must touch the web with respect and dream only dreams of the Soul. Do not dream only of power and riches that the body craves. Real power is not in material things but in the way you present to the world. Present with all of the elements of creation in balance. Otherwise you will feel empty and dead.'*

"I hope all you people are listening to Ningrapo's learning and beg the Mysteries for his understanding," Sinequan said. Her seasoned fingers continued to probe the carving on the stick. "He isn't finished. Listen my children."

*'The soul can experience suffering – but never destruction. Without a Soul the body is useless. To be with a Soul is to know that nothing but our attitude separates us from the rest of creation. In that knowing is where the real power is. Make your dreams ones of what you can give, not what you can get or take. From those fantasies will be born feathers that will fly you home like the mighty eagles.'* Sinquan's breath caught in her throat and a tear escaped from her closed eyelids.

*I had carried my home, my heart, with me – sometimes on my back denying its heaviness. Sometimes I threw it on the forgiving earth, kicked and clawed it and sometimes I abandoned it in my shame. Still Grandfather patiently waited, knowing I could do nothing but return, and leave this message for you to help change the thinking of the world.*

The tribe nuzzled closer; some reached out and grabbed another's hand as Sinequan continued. A grin now danced around the wrinkles on her face.

*'Every person, every plant, every animal and stone has a story. For every twig that falls from a branch, there is someone's story. Just as you*

*collect twigs to start your fires, you must gather the stories of the world. As carefully as you lay your twigs, you must listen to their stories. The warmth from that fire will then settle in your bones as compassion and understanding for each other. Let a flame always burn in your heart for the brothers and sisters of the earth.*

A warm summer wind stirred the fire and sparkles exploded into the silken darkness. The mood of the tribe was trance-like as Ningrapo's spirit moved among them. They slowly began to chant and dance as one, stamping their feet to the staccato of his words.

"Grow the fire, the air, the earth and water - passion and reason, strength and compassion - meet the world with respect and care - feathers are fantasies - leaves are loves - pebbles are poetry - twigs are tales - sticks are stories - connect with knowing - all is one - heart is home– soul is here."

Ningrapo's spirit was not quite satisfied. *"Perhaps we should now teach them the mystery held within a name,"* he whispered in Sinequan's ear. She nodded knowingly and while her people danced and sang, the old blind woman scratched the letters that made up Ningrapo's name in the powdery dirt...

NINGRAPO

or

NORAPING

The notes of the tribe's song reached beyond the rainbow and made Grandfather smile. He could finally close both his eyes.

*Some messages come to us from times past*

*and in mysterious ways.*

*However*

*messages about life, love and learning*

*are being delivered to us*

*in every moment.*

*So I wondered why so many go unnoticed*

*or are simply ignored.*

*Apparently some messages*

*need to be hand-delivered!*

*GM*

## TWELVE STEPS

Monique licked the chocolate from her fingers, sucking each one into her mouth. She let her tongue linger over the stubborn bits and watched the street below. She could hear the bike coming, long before it would flash past.

Dressed entirely in funeral black Frederick was obsessed with speed and kept up his determined pedalling despite the downward slope.

Monique wiped her fingers on her jeans and picked up the gun.

"Soon it will be over *mon cherie,*" she whispered, and noted the height of the steps that spiralled from her room down to the street. Dreamlike she began a deliberate chant.

"Twelve stone steps; twelve disciples; twelve signs of the zodiac; twelve months of the year, twelve tribes of Israel; twelve black and twelve white pyramids in the Egg of Osiris; twelve days of Christmas." Monique pressed her palm against her chest, wincing as yesterday bruises complained. "And there are twelve petals of the heart chakra Frederick," she sobbed. The gunmetal felt deliciously cool in Monique's hot hand.

"Today is 12th of 12th 2012. A good day to die don't you think?"

The tyres on Frederick's bike were squeaking on the bends further up the hill. Monique swallowed the nausea rising in her throat and let her breath carry her words to the street below.

"12 is a standing teacher and a kneeling student. But who is whom, *mon cherie*? You say I just won't learn – that you must punish me – well perhaps Frederick, *I* am the teacher."

Monique negotiated the twelve steps to the street below, listening for the sound of Frederick's bike. She stood in the centre of the road in the place she had watched him hurtle around the bed, endless times. He saw her at the exact moment she pulled the trigger. His bike careered, spinning out of control before crashing.

\*\*\*

Frederick couldn't go to Monique's funeral.

"Poor man," said the surgeon "He will never walk again."

*Life itself is the teacher and our lessons come in many forms.*
*We can avoid some things by acting instantly ...like dodging a bullet.*

*But...*

   *other things happen so slowly we don't perceive*
*the lesson until it is too late.*
*So I wondered ...*

   *if we knew what our next lesson was to be, would*
*we act with wisdom and intelligence or choose to*
*keep our head in the sand?*

   *Some people just won't accept change it seems... so*
*a wise one in the form of a child can come calling.*

*GM*

# DAM DEATH

Summer this year in Australia was brutal. Mother Nature had lifted her green skirts early, leaving in view the nakedness of her sunburnt earth. The grove of trees where Lewis spent much of his time was shaded by eucalypts and the dam still had plenty of water from the spring rains. It was a cool sanctuary of sorts for Lewis. Some might say a 'laboratory' rather than a sanctuary, but like all great minds that take solace in their experiments, Lewis, would definitely agree with the idea of it being his 'laboratory'. The walk from the house over the hill to his laboratory was a scorching crunch of dead grass under his feet, with no shade until he came down from the hilltop to the cool of the grotto.

Breakfast this morning had been bacon and eggs, which was standard fare for Lewis's grandparents. "Grandfather, are you aware of what global warming means to the planet?" Lewis paused with fork mid-air.

"Jesus Lew! Why can't you call me 'Pop' like other kids?" Grandfather McClellan worried his grandson was 'not normal'.

"'Pop sounds like a bubble or balloon bursting. Is that what you what me to think of you - busted?" Lewis half-grinned. Then with an impersonation of an American accent he said, "or maybe you'd like me to think of you as soda-pop?"

Grandmother and Grandfather both shook their heads and looked at each other with disbelief.

"Of course soda-pop would not be suitable," Lewis continued, oblivious to their expressions. "It is complete garbage, full of dangerous chemicals and causes obesity. And Grandfather, you are definitely not garbage! Uninformed perhaps, but not garbage."

"Geez, thanks mate." John McLellan let out a long sigh like the air out of a tyre, and asked his wife how the bloody hell did their son have a boy like this.

"I reckon the stork dropped him at the wrong house, love." Her sigh matched her husband's deflating tyre.

"You two do know that babies are a product of intercourse by a man and woman, not something delivered by a bird?" Asked Lewis, pushing his chair away from the table. His bewildered grandparents closed their eyes.

"Thank you for breakfast Grandma. I've got to get to the water hole while the light is at the right angle. I was certain I saw something in there yesterday that needs investigating."

"Clean your teeth young man!" Amy McClellan yelled after him.

"Oops forgot!" Lewis smiled and then said perhaps if scientists had been able to prove the connection between mouth bacteria and heart disease years ago, perhaps Uncle Charlie would still be alive. Then with a cheeky face he added, "And if your parents had told you to clean your teeth you might still have them."

Impulsively his grandfather ran his tongue over his false teeth. "If I didn't love him so much I'd smack that little buggar's arse!"

The light on the water hole revealed what lay below the surface.

A face, with dark eyes wide open, stared upward into the boy's. Lew's composure was unruffled. He saw himself as an Australian Sherlock, deeply identifying with the genius television character who had uncanny attention to detail.

Lew's persona on Facebook was 'Sherlock' but his father, Paul, in Melbourne, knew nothing of his foray into the social-media.

A yabbie crawled from the mouth of the face in the water, and Lew said, "Hmm, definitely dead." He found a stick and began to gently clear the dead leaves away from the neck and chest area of the corpse. That's when he saw the rope around its neck.

Before bed that night, in stifling country heat, Lewis asked his grandfather if he could visit the neighbouring properties.

"I spose'," said John McLellan. "But it's too bloody hot to walk mate. I could drive over, if we made it early."

"Thanks Grandpa, I'd really like that."

"The Wilsons are away, but the Fenshaws will be up and about early, we'll go to their place," John McClellan said more to himself than anybody else.

That night Lewis was restless, not only because of the heat, but because he was anxious to get on with his investigation of the body in the dam.

It was 8.35am when the two McLellans left their farm in John's truck. By the time he had answered Lewis's first question they were driving over the cattle grid into Fenshaw's dairy farm.

"Do you come here often Grandfather?"

"Yeah y'know - local barbies, celebrations and the like. Nice people."

A massive galvanised shed, as big as an airport hanger dominated the view and black and white cows milled around in pens on the outside. Lewis guessed the number at two hundred and fifty.

"Come on Lew, I'll show'ya how milkin's done these days." John McLellan strode into the shed yelling, "Where are ya mate?" Dallas, you there?"

A short, red-faced, stocky man appeared from around the milking apparatus that filled the shed. Lewis immediately sensed a murderous character, but unfazed, extended his hand to shake when introduced. He liked to get impressions from touching things. This touch confirmed his first impression of Dallas Fenshaw.

The adults talked about the weather, the markets and their families, leaving Lewis to go exploring - or rather investigating.

"Ask me any questions about the milking game, if you want Lewis," called Dallas after the boy.

"Thank you," Lewis called back, but to himself he thought it wasn't a game; dairy-farming was for real.

By the time Lewis and his grandfather arrived back at John's farm for Grandma's scones and tea, the sun's rays were at the wrong angle to see into the depths of the dam. Lewis was patient, knowing if he stayed calm and methodical in his approach, the dead body would reveal to him who was responsible.

"So what d'ya think of dairy-farming mate?" John sucked on his coffee.

"It seems pretty bloody cruel to me", said Lewis. Amy glared at her grandson.

"Watch your language young man, you're only 13!"

"Sorry Grandma, country life seems to be rubbing off on me," he grinned, "but I think there is something about dairy farms you should know." The grin slid from Lew's face and he swallowed, making his adolescent voice box rise and fall in his throat.

"I don't know where to start really."

The grandparents shot each other a look, unsure of what was going to happen next. Lewis took a deep breath and began his discourse. The longer he spoke the more impassioned he became. He spoke of the amount of methane from burping cows contributing to green house grasses. He explained how much water is needed to grow food for cows that people eat - over fifteen thousand litres of water to put just one kilo of meat on a beast. Not to mention the pasture that could grow enough food to feed thousands instead of a hundred. "But worst of all," Lewis sucked in his breath ready for the next eruption of information - information that had his grandparents staring at each other in disbelief.

"Did you know that the only way a cow can have milk in her udder is to have a baby? Of course you did. But the bloody Farmers, sorry grandma, don't want to give the milk to little babies - no - they want to sell it to make money! So they, they... rip the calves away from their mother's who then spend months crying for their lost babies!"

Lewis stood, grabbed the last scone and said, "Oh! There is much more that people don't know. It's sickening. But I've got to get on with my investigation. Thank you for the scones Grandma."

His Apple Mac laptop would need rebooting. "Bloody slow internet in the country," he said as he parked in front of it, ready to extend the fingers of his curiosity.

The next morning he loped down the dry hillside eagre to stare into those dead, dark eyes of the corpse again. Wary brown ducks glided swiftly away from the newcomer, while a frill-necked lizard watched, frozen to his rock. Lewis picked up the stick and continued moving the silt and leaves off the corpse, talking to himself the whole time in Sherlock style. "Brown coat, but that's not certain, it may be coloured by the mud. Impossible to ascertain the age, but the body's big enough to be an adult. Big-breasted female by the looks of it. No shoes. Hmmm looks like a tattoo - a number or a code of some sort? Almost looks like a hieroglyph. Ah! An earring! Mmmm, just one ear and with same hieroglyph." He drew the design in the mud at the edge of the dam, committing it to memory. "I've seen this somewhere before. Think Lewis, think."

In a light bulb moment Lewis galloped up the hill toward the house.

"Just in time for lunch, love," said his grandmother Amy. "Wash your hands."

Lunch was a toasted cheese and tomato sandwich - one of Lewis's favourites. John arrived, wiped the sweat from his face on a grimy handkerchief and they all tucked in.

"I've got to see Dallas about something Lew, wanna come with me?"

"Oh! Grandfather, you have no idea how much I want to go back to that dairy farm." Lewis could hardly sit still as if electric shocks pulsated through his young body. John grinned and said, "Well promise to call me 'Pop' when we're there, and I'll let you."

"Done deal...Pop."

Dinner that night was something Lew's grandparents would never forget. Lew's face was grave, but he was self-assured as he spoke.

"I've got something to tell you, that might be a bit shocking. But you need to know this before I go back to Melbourne."

His grandparents were used to his 'revelations', and as always they locked glances and wondered what was next.

"I found a body in the dam!"

Amy's hand flew to her face so John took the reins.

"Go on, son."

"At first I thought it was murder and I was certain I knew who the murderer was. But now I know it was suicide, although my suspected murderer is still responsible." Despite their bewilderment, Amy and John had no chance of interrupting. Lewis continued as if in a court of Law. "I thought it was murder when I saw the rope around her neck, but after I finished my identification - the tattoo on the body and an ear ring in the right ear, both with the same inscription - I realised it was suicide." He gulped from his water glass, wiped the sweat from his upper lip on his arm and continued unabated. "I conclude this was a young mother, whose child was taken from her soon after birth by an evil, self-serving, unconscionable man. She searched, crying in vain for weeks, perhaps longer, then finally threw herself into the dam to end her pain."

Tears we trickling down Lewis's face. His grandmother reached over and wiped them away.

"How do you know all this, love," she said gently.

Lewis swallowed and said he had identified the inscription on her tattoo and earring. John, nonplussed, mumbled about the bloody Internet filing kid's heads with rubbish. Lewis spoke slowly and deliberately.

"It wasn't the Internet Grandpa, I did my own, on the ground, investigation. The inscriptions where the same as all the other cows in that mongrel Renshaw's herd. The brown coat threw me for a while because his cows are black and white, but today I asked him if he ever had brown cows and he admitted he did. That poor mother cow killed herself in your dam because she couldn't bear the separation from her baby. I'm going to my room now. Thank you for dinner Grandma, but just so you know, from now on I will never eat meat or dairy again."

The phone rang on the kitchen bench and Amy spoke to her son John about the dead cow in the dam, ear-tags and brands, and Lew's imagination.

"I know it's hard Mum, but that's the way Lewis deals with the fact that his mother abandoned him. He needs to believe she wanted him more than anything and would kill herself because he was taken from her. He can't accept it was the drugs."

"Is that Dad?" Lewis stood in pyjamas after his shower and took the phone from Amy.

"Just so you know Dad, I've become a Vegan. What people do to animals is beyond belief. And what meat farming is doing to the planet is horrific."

"That's fantastic Lew, I've waited years to hear you say that. Let's help save the planet kiddo. Guess what? I've just had solar panels installed."

Amy kissed her grandson goodnight and went to watch T.V.

"Goodnight Grandma. Y'know you don't have to be psychic to see the future. Just awake." Lewis switched on his computer, waited for the connection and searched 'emissions from coal-fired power stations.'

But that's another story...........

*It is believed by many*
*    that a Psychic can see the future;*
*that an Oracle can tell your fortune*
*    and that Clairvoyants have powers*
*        which ordinary people don't have,*
*    so I wondered if that was really true?*

*What if those of us with so-called 'powers' simply*
*had a profound understanding of their own psyche,*
*which enabled them to have perfect empathy with*
*another's?*

*If that were so, then why don't we all have such*
*insight? Is it possible that our ego is so dominant*
*that we miss the signs, even our own ones? This story*
*shows how easily that could happen....*

*GM*

## SIRENS OF KARMA

*JERRY*

When I read the note written in my wife's familiar scrawl I never imagined how my life was about to change.

*"My one true love, you always did what I asked of you, so now that I've gone, please, please take the attached ticket and go to New Zealand on this bus tour. Something very precious awaits you."*

Georgina, my love of thirty years, had died some months ago and I had become a hermit-like shadow wading through a swamp of loss and grief. She was an accomplished Psychic and I was an accomplished Sceptic. Georgie had predicted her own death, so in reverence for this woman that I loved so unashamedly, despite our differing views on metaphysics, I went to New Zealand's south island. Sitting behind me on the bus, two people were engrossed in conversation.

"I'm told that you are psychic," he stated disdainfully.

My ears, longing for Georgina and her sensitivity, reached hungrily for the other's answer.

"It's not that I'm psychic so much, as an interpreter of signs," she answered. "When a snail cements its gummy foot to my laundry wall high above my head I know that when the rain starts it will be unrelenting and flooding. Ants become more obsessive-compulsive than usual then, running faster than wild stallions, in and out of their nest at these times. If you listen you can hear the firing of their orders – staccato Morse-code-like commands to each other – 'quickly for the Queen's sake move it!' Nature unfailingly communicates with itself."

His voice took on an air of superiority.

"I have to say, I'm a complete sceptic," he drawled.

Unperturbed, she continued. "Four-footed things move to high ground long before human instruments register a coming tsunami and curiously, we too tend to move to the high moral and *oral* ground in denial of our emotional tsunamis. Verbosity can be such a clever camouflage for those who can't recognise signs."

I was stunned. This could have been my Georgie talking.

"That's all very well m'dear," he mumbled. "But tell me how the hell do you explain some of these wild claims that you 'believers' make."

I wanted her to trounce this intellectual wanker so much I was squirming in my seat. Then her calm, intelligent answer had me secretly cheering.

"The fish in the tsunami know that their world will be whipped like cream and slathered roughly over caked earth, but helpless, they are still left gasping on that land after the water returns to the deep. So it is with me. Both of us swimming in something much larger than ourselves and knowing of our fate doesn't always bring us joy. Sometimes it does. The signs might also whisper of greatness or shout of ecstasy and safety."

"I don't follow," he frowned.

I knew exactly what she meant. Georgie would be so proud of me. A shy grin played among my wrinkles as the girl continued.

"I can read these signs and like a ship's Captain with my licked finger in the breeze, know which way to turn the sails. And sometimes I don't know. Perhaps there is no breeze in that moment of questioning or I've had a cataclysm of my own, beyond my control, that sweeps away all order so that I lose my bearings. At other times clouds hide the stars - my map that shows my place in the universe - and I have to wait for them to clear."

"You're referring to astrology I suppose? Total bullshit. No proof whatsoever."

I hoped his rudeness wouldn't freeze her out. He was so intent in making her wrong that he wasn't present to her beautiful analogy at all. She calmly continued as though he wasn't even there.

"Sometimes there are moments of such unsurpassed vision and clarity I'm left stunned - times when the pupil of another's eye draws me into it's blackness and falling down the well of their own knowing I tumble, scraping myself on their walls. Wanting it to be over I draw strength from my own well of wisdom to pull me out. Then I can come up with a bucket of diamonds for us both. It's all about reading the signs."

The bus drew into a parking bay near the Franz Joseph Glacier.

"So, is this so-called ability that you have, inherited?" he sneered, as everyone prepared to exit.

"I believe I get it from my mother."

"Didn't I hear you say yesterday that you were adopted? So you know your biological parents then?" He was in more comfortable territory now.

"I've never met them. My mother was very young, sixteen, when I was conceived. Now I'm orphaned again. My adopted parents were killed in a car accident last year."

"Oh! My dear, what rotten luck. Ha! Lucky you can talk to the spirit-world eh?"

I thought he was an insensitive bastard and didn't hear her answer as we fell out of the bus into brilliant light, smoothing wrinkled clothes and shouldering cameras. She looked mystifyingly familiar as I watched her exit the bus, one delicate hand on her pregnant belly. She was perhaps thirty-five, small and serious-looking with kind emerald eyes. Like yaks wandering the Himalayas, our troupe ambled along to the foot of the glacier, all entranced by the wonder of this river of ice, grinding its way to sea level.

Lost in my grief, wishing that Georgie and I were hand in hand as always, I felt a touch on my arm. Moist emerald eyes smiled gently into my red-rimmed ones.

"I'm feeling your pain, but I want you to know that Georgina is here with you now...with us."

"I heard what you said to that...that... insensitive pig on the bus," I babbled. "My wife was psychic also and I was a sceptic."

"*Was* a sceptic?"

"How you explained your gift is so..." I grappled for words and started to cry. "How did you know about Georgie?" The words gagged in my mouth while embarrassingly large amounts of water flowed down my cheeks.

The little psychic slipped a soft hand into mine.

"I *know* because I found her just before she died. Georgina was my birth mother and we wrote to each other. She sent you here so that we could meet."

Confused, I was struck absurdly dumb.

"Even if I couldn't meet *her*," she squeaked, stifling her tears, "I'm here to meet my father."

Overwhelmed I couldn't comprehend what she was saying.

"Are you saying that I'm your father?" My heart started to thump against my ribs.

"No sweet man. That 'insensitive pig' apparently is. He's the famous playwright, Carter Wallace. Have you heard of him in Australia?"

I shook my head as this angelic little woman continued. "Don't concern yourself with him. His karma is his own creation." She squeezed my hand and grinned a smile so familiar that I shook with emotion.

"Georgina said my intuition would lead me to a wonderful man who would be delighted to be my stepfather," she said. "I'm Kylie. You *are* Jerry aren't you?"

\*\*\*

*CARTER WALLACE*

"Carter my darling," try writing a play about murder, Angelique' whispered. "You never know it might be the very thing to get you rolling again."

A sickening feeling that I'd never write again gnawed in my guts like rats on a carcass, as I trawled through old works for inspiration.

"Rolling eh?" I smiled wryly, a small constriction squeezing my throat. 'Rolling' was our euphemism for sex. She would be completely thunderstruck later that night.

"I just found this poem I wrote before we met," I said, "about the rigors of writing, but I damn-well can't seem to write about anything at all now, never mind another play."

She brought me tea and I read her my handwritten poem, with a voice that was weirdly slow.

*REJECTION SLIPS by Carter Wallace*
*Writing is mountaineering of a kind.*
*Every step helps us find our destiny*
> *Taking us to impossible heights*
> *in freezing temperatures that makes us sweat*
*with dogged determination,*
*or smile in rapture at unspeakable beauty.*
> *Prising, gauging the feeling from each step,*
> *we hammer pegs into the rock of time –*
> *creating footholds on a mountain of words,*
*ages old.*
*Poetry is precarious as hanging on a rope*
*or standing on a bluff a million footprints high-*
> *wind slinging sleet at your exposed face*
> *and pushing so hard on your chest you feel your heart thumping.*
*One careless footstep, a slip – a bloody slip*
> *then you'll fall to a wordless death.*
> *No-one will care or remember.*
*Because they won't know your name.*

*Or instead of bouncing off the crag*
*like a dropped book amid mortified gasps,*
> *do you tug on your ripcord and after the shock*
> *of being snatched from flight,*
*does relief flood your senses*
*softening your fixed-eyed stare?*
*Do you land disoriented at the base of your ego,*
*again to conjure words with no carelessness,*
> *while you climb the bluff again?*

*How fragile we are. We forget we can fly.*

Angelique kissed me then - soft, wet and lingering kisses - burbling through our meshed faces until I laughed too.

"My love," she said, "you must take your own advice and remember that you *can* fly. And now *we* must fly or we will miss the opening of your play!"

The theatre was full when we arrived with a few media people milling in the foyer, eager for an interview.

"Mr Wallace! Carter! Could we have a quick word? What was your inspiration for 'Rugged'? How long did you work on it? Is this the first time you've seen it acted, Mr Wallace? Does this have a similar theme as your other plays?"

The lights dimmed in the theatre so Angelique told them I'd give them some time during intermission. She was so beautiful. My young muse. Her eyes glistened with their special mystery even in the dark.

"I'm so proud of you Darling," she giggled and blew hot air into my ear after we were seated.

The play was spectacular, but the brilliance of the lines I'd written, made me feel even more insecure. How would I ever repeat the same quality of work again? I had no words left in me. I was fragile *and* I couldn't fly. The actors were talented, often outstanding; the sets were extraordinary and the applause was thunderous but I felt empty somehow.

During Intermission's crush of journalists, Angelique told them that I wasn't feeling well and that we'd do a phone interview tomorrow. Then she pressed vodka into my hand and told me to throw it back as she had another ready to go. By the third drink I was more relaxed and then we were back inside, waiting in anticipation for the final scene. I was remarkably calm for someone who knew what was about to happen. The actors said every syllable as I imagined it. The male lead, whom I'd called Arturio, swept up Cassandra the female lead, as easily as picking up a child.

"Oh!" she gasped. "What are you doing?"

"I'm taking you to my bed, little One!"

"No, no!" Cassandra was panting. "Let us lie here on this astonishing red rug."

Sighs of women could be heard throughout the dark theatre. Arturio laid Cassandra with great care and gentleness on the rug. He dramatically swept back her voluminous hair exposing his lover's sensuous throat. The audience were mesmerised.

"You are too beautiful my Angel. Beauty like yours should be captured before it withers and fades." Arturio scanned Cassandra's face as if intent on committing her features to memory. Then a millisecond before the curtain fell with a thud, he swept a knife across his beauty's throat.

***

Ironically your body was found rolled in a red rug Angelique. If you had come with me on the bus tour, perhaps you'd still be mine. The day I returned home began ordinarily, yet to me it was normal as fingernail grime and equally ugly, because again you had stayed out all night. I had no way of predicting what the day would reveal, except for a sense of unease that constricted my throat. Small and insignificant annoyances continued until 2.10pm. Burning toast. A fly fretting against the glass. The fire going cold. The phone sitting mute on my desk, giving no argument that I would never see you again. The time is engraved on my memory, because that was when the police said you'd been found. Have you seen this red rug before they said. No I said. Take your time; perhaps you've seen it on someone's floor, somewhere, he said. I drifted off then, tracing countless steps on endless carpets – red carpets – red patterned carpets – plain red carpets – dirty carpets – new, clean carpets. My throat closed shut, so I shook my head no, pushing through air as thick as jelly.

Lying on the bed later, much later, drugged witless I dreamt of a magic red carpet that flew us to exotic lands. We sailed on exhilarating currents in passionate ecstasy to the Great Pyramids and up the Nile. Crimson - that colour of daring, lust and adventure – held us aloft. We sailed like albatross on trade winds to Turkey, Greece and Italy, entranced with everything as lovers are. Yet we were weirdly disconnected from it all, because every one of our senses was in bondage to each other – only to each other.

A red rug they said. The red could well be my own blood, drained from my veins as you died, taking my reason for living with you. Albatross mate for life – I am bloodless, lifeless without you.

How fragile we are. We forget that we can fly. But Angelique', you were my wings.

***

"What's happened here Constable?"

"Looks like the old man has slashed his wrists, Sir. He'd lost so much blood, by the time he was found, there was no chance. Ugh! As you can see the entire rug has turned red."

"Do we know who he is? Next of kin?"

"Carter Wallace, the playwright. His girlfriend was murdered about two weeks ago. Seemingly no children or family."

"Is he a suspect in her death?"

"No Sir, it's been established he was on a bus in the south island at the time of death."

## KYLIE and GEORGINA

Jerry wiped remnants of food from his face. "Have you chosen a name for your baby?" He smiled discretely, not wanting to show blatant excitement at the prospect of sharing in Georgina's grandchild.

"Mmm. I'm compelled to call her Cassandra." Kylie took Jerry's plate to the sink. "Do you like that name?"

"Cassandra was the beautiful princess of Troy," Jerry told her.

The god Apollo apparently was entranced by her and wanted to possess her, but Cassandra wasn't convinced she wanted him as her lover. Do you know about this ancient Greek myth?"

"Keep going Jerry, I'm fascinated!" Kylie wriggled in little girl fashion.

"Well, to entice her into his bed, he offered her the gift of prophecy and then rather like a mentor he taught her how to use her gift. However she still refused to surrender her body to him, which made him rather angry, so he decided to punish her.

"Mmmm not a nice god." Kylie stared off into the ether. "I'm told from Georgina, that men who make woman and children cry are to be feared, because that is what destroys civilization."

Jerry stiffened, wrestling with his scepticism of ghosts and spectres, yet wanting Georgina to be there with him. Continuing, he said, "Apollo put a curse on Cassandra that still allowed her to see the future, but the curse made everyone believe she was deliberately lying. Whenever she tried to warn friends of their fate, no one believed her. To their detriment and to her torment."

"Hmm I wonder why I thought 'Cassandra' would be perfect for my baby? Perhaps it's a karmic thing. Let's sleep on it Jerry."

Jerry hugged her warmly. He expected Georgina's smell, the same softness of womanly breasts over his heart and the sense of familiarity, but nothing was the same. Kylie was shorter, bonier and smelt only of the curry she had cooked. Yet her eyes revealed the same holographic mystery that reflected him back to himself. Lost in their own longing for Georgina, both their eyes misted as they said goodnight.

In her room Kylie gently open her mother's last letter again.. Georgina's writing was uncannily like her own.

*My precious Angel,*
*The photos you sent do you little justice. I know because for thirty-four years my spirit-breath has lifted soft curls from your beautiful face*

*and I swam in the deep pools of your knowing eyes. I have kissed your sleeping eyelids and walked in your waking footsteps. Our souls will always sing divine melodies together.*

*Soon your biological father, Carter Wallace will no longer walk in a body. I warned him his life would end badly but he just saw it as a threat. My solicitors, Luscombe and Mereweather in Australia, will contact you as Carter's only beneficiary. They hold your birth certificate and a letter that I made him sign when he forced me to give you away.*

*"How can I possibly write with a child running around?" he said.*

*He forgot that with focus we could fly! Now he leaves you the means to fly in comfort Kylie dear.*

*Jerry is a special soul. We simply adore each other. He will be a sensitive and loving grandfather to all your children, but I suspect if you tell him that I am the life kicking in your belly, it may well do his head in. He can be such a sceptic. I trust that you will show him the signs and gently lead him into his own mystical awakening.*

*See you soon.*

*With boundless love, I am your Georgina...*

*(...once called Cassandra. Jerry can tell you that legend.)*

*Legends are littered with dead heroes,*
*so I wondered*
*where are they now?*
*And what of the ones*
*who walk quietly among us,*
*like the two young men in the next story?*

GM

# NO GRATITUDE IN APRIL

Humans can have a skewed way of looking at the world. We say the sun *rises*, but it does not rise. The earth spins on its axis *toward* the sun in a perfect rotation. This day was no different, but a human rotation or at least a spinning was about to occur.

The Print Shop sat above the coffee shop, which was a blessing for the three women, April, Mae and June, who worked there. Private phone calls could be made and taken while on a lunch or morning tea break.

"Can I see you tonight, my boyfriend is home, but I can find an excuse," whispered June the junior staff member. June was Filipino and like many from those islands used an Anglo-Saxon name.

"I really must talk to you. My brother was killed by the President for the drugs, but how else could he support his family? I'm scared if I go home to see my family I won't be allowed back in to Australia." Turning her head away from other diners, June wiped the tears that slipped from her eyes then gasped into the phone. "Please God no!" She choked. "Are they really likely to cancel my visa? This government is getting more like the Philippines!"

June screamed when a hand pressed on her shoulder and with a gasp spun around to see Mae-Lin, the manager of The Print Shop. Mae-Lin was born in Sydney from Chinese-Malay parents and was a brilliant entrepreneur.

"Sweet girl, what ever is wrong?" She pulled out a chair and sat. "You can tell me anything, you know. Can I help?"

June's dark eyes were pleading and her pupils were giant black chasms in her beautiful face. "I'm scared my visa will be cancelled and I will not be allowed to live here anymore. Did you know the government wants to cancel my visa?"

June's small brown hand was cold and sweaty to Mae-Lin's touch. "No, I did not know that," she said. "Whatever would I do without you June."

"But I don't think April likes me," blurted the distraught girl. Mae-Lin's kind smile did little to comfort June.

"April doesn't like anyone, because she doesn't like herself, June. Let me make a phone call," Mae-Lin said, "I'll see what I can do."

Meanwhile another situation was unfolding in the office upstairs. April was close to retirement and had been a bookkeeper all her life. April had experienced her share of misfortune like most people, but nothing in the extreme. Yet like June she was filled with fear and it had become her normal way of functioning - fear of the dark, fear of spiders, fear of burglary, fear of strangers, fear of accidents, fear of the unknown and especially fear of Moslems. A poster on the wall above her desk read:

*The most effective prison is the one*
*you don't know you're in.*
*By Gurdjeiff, Armenian Philosopher.*

Yet people wiser than herself did not influence April. She knew what she knew, and she knew she wanted Australia to be like the Australia she grew up in.

Sadly, April lacked enough self-esteem to become fearless and embrace change. She also lacked friendships because she was fundamentally boring and self-righteous. Her most frequent conversations were in her own head, which uncannily she mastered while doing the book-keeping for The Print Shop. *That silly Filipino girl! She still doesn't know how to make a decent cup of tea. How can the boss of an Australian company be Asian? It's not right. This is a white country - we got where we are on decent Australian values. How could we ever let Moslems in here? They are evil and want to take over the world.*

With the office empty of prying eyes, she logged onto the White Supremists website and with nodding head, and a hungry heart she read the latest post. 'Please enter your email and phone number if you'd like to be included in our rallies for a better Australia.' So she did. Immediately she heard the 'ding' of incoming mail. 'G'day April,' it read, would you be interested in a meeting with members from your suburb tonight?' April thought for a while, then answered 'yes please' and hit 'send'. The reply came saying she would get a phone call later in the day to confirm the meeting. Suddenly the world seemed better to April. She had found her 'tribe'.

Later that day the phone on Mae-Lin's desk rang and June worried about her visa, stopped breathing, but Mae-Lin waved her a 'don't worry' so she went back to sorting piles of printed flyers. The phone call over, Mae-Lin told June and April they would be required to stay and work late that night as they had an urgent deadline for one of their biggest jobs yet.

"Of course," said June, "I just need to tell my friend, OK?"

Mae-Lin ran her perfectly manicured fingers through her black hair as her managerial mind began planning the events to come. "Why don't you girls take an extra 15 minutes for afternoon tea and sort out this evening then." Then with a wink at June she said, "I've got an important call to make now."

April's plans were dashed in that moment and her self-talk was verging on insanity. *This isn't fair. It's not right. I have an important meeting to go to. If I didn't need to work for three more years to get the pension I'd bloody well tell this Moslem cow to shove her job. I hope they ring me during afternoon tea. What'll I tell them? I'll probably be here 'till 10 o'clock - is that too late? By the time I get back to the northern beaches it'll be much later - Oh! God, I hate her.*

April's phone rang while she waited for her afternoon order of coffee and very non-Australian Greek baklava.

"This is Philip, about the meeting tonight April." After a few moments of nervousness, April found the caller delightful and they chatted like old school chums. He asked her where she worked and told her not to worry, as there would be plenty of other White Supremists meetings.

"Perhaps you and I could meet for coffee in the meantime," said Philip. Alice's heart skipped a beat.

"Yes, yes! How wonderful. There is a coffee shop under my office, what a shame it will be closed when I finish tonight. But there is a lovely park opposite, maybe we could get a take-a-way and sit in the park sometime."

Philip asked her where it was and she gave him a ridiculously long explanation of how to get there.

"Sounds perfect," he said. "I'll be in touch."

April was in a phantasmagorical daze. *Be in touch. Be in touch. Omigod! It's been years since a man has touched me. I wonder what he's like. His voice is a bit raspy so he's probably my age - too perfect. I hope he's taller than me - buggar it, who cares - tall, short - coffee in the park.* Her sighs and smirks caused a few smiles with some patrons thinking perhaps she had dementia. "It's nice to see you smile April," said the Barista. If only he'd known that the smile would be wiped from her face within a few hours.

It was 9.45pm when the three exhausted women left the office. Usually April would have had hammering thoughts all night about the demands made of her as not being part of her job description, but tonight she was in a romantic fantasy.

Mae-Lin knew better than to ask personal questions, while June wondered if April wasn't meeting a man this night. They said goodnight in the car park and April watched the others leave as her phone signalled a message. *'Guess who's waiting in the park with a coffee for you?'* April quickly scanned herself in the mirror, locked the car and walked across the road to the park. The streetlights were bright and she could see a man in a coat, holding a phone. The light from the screen showed him to be only about 45 years old, definitely white Australian, not as handsome as she hoped but he smiled when he saw her, and April's world turned suddenly to fireworks on New Year's Eve.

"I've got our coffee on the seat over there." Philip gestured to a place away from the path. April was entranced and took his arm as though they were already lovers. Then more fireworks exploded as he punched her in the face, then her stomach and dragged her collapsing body into the bushes. She screamed and groaned unable to comprehend what was happening. All her fears came together in the perfect storm.

Mohammed and Yusef were walking home from the mosque when they heard a muffled scream from the park.

"Did you hear that?" said Yusef. Mohammed stopped and turned his good ear to the night sky.

"Yah that was not a duck on the pond, it sounded like a woman."

"There it is again, quick, follow me."

The two young men dragged Philip off April, while screaming, "You low-life, how could you do this, did you think you could get away with this?" They tied his hands and feet together with their belts and Yusef phoned 000.

Mohammed sat beside April and stroked the hair from her face.

"You're OK now ma'm, you're OK now. We got the pig who did this to you." Yusef covered April's nakedness with her skirt, then they prayed to their god for her, and held her hands. April was in such a state of shock, she was grateful and terrified at the same time. *Ew such long black beards on such sweet faces. Why don't they shave - it's so ugly. Such kind eyes. That man could have killed me. These are Muslim boys. This must be a trick - maybe they raped me and said it was Philip. No wait I remember.* April tried to speak, trembling as the memories flooded over her. Mohammed bent closer. "I didn't hear that ma'm. I'm sorry, I am a bit deaf from a bomb blast in my country."

Later in the hospital, the Police told April the man who raped her had probably raped and possibly murdered three other victims, by hacking websites and seeming legitimate. The Counsellor told her, "It's not your fault April, and you are so lucky that Mohammed and Yusef heard your screams, otherwise he might have killed you."

The next day Mohammed and Yusef, bearing flowers and chocolates, stood at the end of April's bed.

"Why are you here?" April felt anxiety rising as she focused on the boy's black beards, nut-brown skin and their accents.

"Just as the earth turns toward the sun each day, we want to encourage you to turn toward the sun too, ma'm." Yusef smiled from his heart.

Morphine evaporated April's usual shyness. "No, I mean why are you here in this country?"

"We have work visas ma'm," Mohammed looked down and swallowed, "but we fear the government will soon cancel them."

Yusef asked April if she would be so kind as to write a letter to the Minister and tell them how they saved her life.

April clenched her teeth, clamped her lips, turned her head and looked at the wall.

The earth still spins toward the sun, yet there are people who have a skewed way of looking at the world and will not embrace the light.

*Some would say to embrace the light, part of us has to die.*

*I wondered if that is true.*
*Perhaps the ego, which defines our personality and the roles we play, has to step into another role.*
*The role of the Soul.*

*But what is that exactly?*
*Our calling? Our purpose?*
*Our destiny or dharma?*

*This can require leaving our current beliefs, dogmas, imprinting and identity behind...but to do that requires a great leap of trust in something far greater than our egoic humanness...*

*a leap into a new life.*

*If we didn't know that a leap toward new life was really a jump toward a death, would we still jump? It certainly seems so.*

*GM*

# THE LEGEND OF THE EAGLE MEDICINE

Many, many, many moons ago in the land of the Redman, a mighty Shaman walked among his people. His name was White Eagle and he possessed great and powerful medicine. He could heal his brothers and speak to all the earth's children...the animal and bird spirits, the water spirits, the spirit of the wind and the Earth mother. White Eagle could hear Father Sky God, the Great Spirit Wakantanka speak to him. The buffalo and bear and eagle were his totems.

White Eagle wore the horns of the buffalo on his proud head and slept in the arms of bear fur at night. His rattle and drum were dressed with feathers of crow and hawk and for ceremony he wore a cloak made from eagle feathers. All these things he did because his father White Cloud knew he was the mightiest Shaman of all their clan, and nurtured White Eagle's gifts.

His Grandfather was called Nanuk and came from the Land of the Midnight Sun. When White Eagle was a small boy, Nanuk told him that he must plant his seed in fertile ground so that the gift of their great medicine would continue after they had passed into spirit.

When White Eagle was a young brave he planted his seed in his one true love and a girl child was born. She was called White Feather and grew to be a powerful medicine woman. She was compassionate and wise and trusted that the Great Spirit would guide her steps.

One day as White Eagle was preparing to leave his body for the last time, he called White Feather to his side.

"You have made our ancestors proud, White Feather. You have made your father proud. I leave you my drum and in return I ask you to give our people a child who will continue the lineage of our medicine. There is no brave suitable for you, but the Great Spirit speaks to me now, saying you will be given a child from the stars, with the eyes of an eagle. Now, my daughter, it is time that I go to the ancestors."

Then White Eagle's spirit slipped quietly from his body.

White Feather sat beside his body, softly drumming into the night, fearing the loss of White Eagle's great presence. Then from somewhere in her soul she heard his voice.

"Go to the desert, White Feather. The Spirit of our ancestors call to you."

Strapping White Eagle's drum to her back, she slipped quietly into the night and looking up at the stars, she shivered, pulling her blanket closer. Her spirit totems, crow, coyote and bear walked with her and she began to howl like the wind. Feeling her Father's spirit engulf her she started to run as though propelled by some invisible force - young woman and totems, howling and flying, running and weeping.

Spent, she fell down and slept. Slept and dreamt. In her dream a magnificent and blinding beam of light fell upon her sleeping body. She opened her swollen eyes and shielding them from the glare, saw a craft above her pouring light into the dark desert night.

"White Feather, come to us, we bring you a gift from the stars."

Slowly she floated upward and was surrounded and supported by beings of the Light.

"Creator of all beings instructs us to complete your initiation," she felt them say, "and so we give you the name MaRai this night to seal your destiny. It means child of the Mighty Sun. You shall from this time shine your magnificence on the children of Earth. You will fear nothing ever again, because MaRai, you are one with us".

Completely enveloped by their love she was laid on a bed, where she drifted into a deep coma.

White Feather awoke in the arms of a sacred mountain, as the first rays of sun stroked her sleeping cheek. She stood and stretched the stiffness from her muscles. High above her on a rocky outcrop a white eagle called to her, "MaRai... MaRai." Her new name echoed in the still morning air, and she knew she did not dream what happened during the night. She was content. White Eagle was still with her and she drummed his drum all the way back to the village of her people.

Soon White Feather realised she had a boy child in her belly and she called the tribe together to tell them what had happened.

The day of the birth was a day of great rejoicing in the tribe and the baby was called Eagle Feather to honour his lineage.

Eagle Feather, even as a boy, showed all the qualities of being a great medicine man. He loved his mother White Feather, never questioning her wisdom and caring for her in every way. They would often go into the desert together and speak to the Earth and Sky Spirits. When they returned, the tribe would thrill at their power and feel proud to have such medicine in their clan.

Eagle Feather and the chief's son, Skilled as a Fox, were of similar age and were great friends. They spent many hours together - Eagle Feather trying to teach Skilled as a Fox the secrets of the earth and stars - Skilled as a Fox trying to prove his manhood by challenging Eagle Feather to competitions of strength and skill.

One moonless night White Feather and her son were many miles away from the tribe, sleeping under the stars. In a deep sleep, Eagle Feather saw a rattlesnake in Skilled as a Fox's bed. He leapt to his feet and ran faster than the wind. His lungs burned, his feet hurt and still he ran until he reached his friend's side. Precisely as the snake was about to strike, Eagle Feather snatched it into his blanket. Then he woke up his friend and told him what happened.

"Ya! You really do have the eyes of an eagle. Let me kill it!" yelled Skilled as a Fox.

"No! It was *you* who rolled on *it*! Why must we take the life of our snake brother?" questioned Eagle Feather.

The next day the boys took the snake into the desert and set it free.

"One day I will be Chief," said Skilled as a Fox, "and you will be Medicine Man. You have saved the life of a Chief. We are now blood brothers, are we not?"

The boys cut their wrists and bound them together with a leather thong to let the bloods intermingle.

"Blood Brothers!" they yelled.

Skilled as a Fox secretly hoped that now he would have some of Eagle Feather's medicine.

2

Many moons passed and Skilled as a Fox was indeed Chief. He was a fearsome and fearless warrior...too young and too proud. He would have done many foolish things, driven by his pride, if it had not been for Eagle Feather's wisdom. Eagle Feather was Medicine Man and his mother, White Feather, was in her prime. Many Nations had heard of their medicine.

Skilled as a Fox's squaw was a beautiful gentle soul with eyes like dark jewels. She'd had no children and Skilled as a Fox was angry that he had no proof of his manhood, so he called her Barren as the Hot Sand.

One day she came to White Feather bruised and bleeding. Skilled as a Fox had beaten her for not giving him a son. The older woman treated the young woman's wounds and gave her healing herbs. When Eagle Feather saw what his blood brother had done he made a decision. He and his mother knew it was not the squaw who was barren, but the Chief.

The medicine of the ancestors had to be passed on and so with Barren as Hot Sand's permission he gave her his seed. In due course, she presented the chief with a daughter, a child with her mother's eyes and her father's medicine. Skilled as a Fox never knew that he was not her real father...and the child's father, Eagle Feather, went to join the ancestors before he could tell her.

Skilled as a Fox took another wife, and another, in desperate pursuit of a son; a warrior he would be proud of. He became increasingly angry as the years passed.

## 3

Many seasons of drought had taken toll their on the tribe. The hunting grounds were poor and many had died of sickness, including Barren as Hot Sand. White Feather was now old and frail. Warriors of the Crow Nation plotted to capture Eagle Feather and his medicine by taunting Skilled as a Fox into war. His pride was made greater by his anger.

"We cannot possibly win a battle, my brother," Eagle Feather said. "We are weak from little food and our numbers are small. The Crow are vicious warriors. We cannot fight. We must not fight. We will all die!"

"We WILL fight. We WILL win!" snarled Skilled as a Fox. "We will ask our relations from across the mountains to join with us. They are also small in number and will welcome the invitation. My daughter Dancing Bird will marry their Chief's son. It will work. We will fight!"

Eagle Feather was shocked. His daughter must not marry just *anybody*. She carried the medicine of the Eagle Clan.

"We must let her marry only if the brave is worthy, my friend.

To marry a chief's daughter, the brave must be a mighty warrior, yes?" he ventured.

"What you say is true, blood brother. You will devise a test for him. If he fails, we will go to war without them! I have spoken!"

Eagle Feather prayed to Wakantanka for help. He was on trial as much as the young brave and felt a sickness in his belly at the responsibility. His power animals, cougar, wolf, eagle and crow gathered around him to comfort his spirit.

A powwow was called and it was agreed that the son and daughter of the Chiefs would join the clans by marriage, only if the young brave, Skulking Wolf, returned from the vision quest that Eagle Feather would initiate.

From the moment Skulking Wolf and Dancing Bird saw each other the passion was great between them. The women took Dancing Bird to the wedding tent and prepared her. Eagle Feather took Skulking Wolf into his tepee and began the vision quest. The young brave drank the potion mixed by the Shaman, then lay on the bearskin rug. While Eagle Feather chanted, danced and rattled around him, Skulking Wolf left his body and began to journey into the astral realms. The Shaman followed the brave into the Spirit World as his wolf totems howled a mournful wail. Eagle Feather stayed well back as this was a test to see if the brave was worthy of his daughter. Soon Skulking Wolf came to a river. On the opposite bank were water nymphs who called seductively to him.

"Come to us lover, we will care for you, we will love you. Come to us. Come to us."

If the brave crossed the river he would not be able to return to his body - he would die. There would be no wedding. Dancing Bird would be shattered. The tribe would all be killed in battle with the Crow. Eagle Feather would have failed. He had to leave enough time for Skulking Wolf to be tested and yet he was afraid that if he left too much time it would be too late. He used all his medicine to call him back, but Skulking Wolf was weak willed and drifted into death with the water nymphs.

Eagle Feather left the astral realms and with heavy heart and pain in his eyes he went to the bridal tent. Grandfather's buffalo headdress seemed heavy and bowed his head. His once broad, erect shoulders rounded under his cloak of eagle feathers as he told Dancing Bird there would be no wedding. Her screams pierced the night and into his heart. He felt his mother's touch on his arm.

"Come my son," she said as she gestured toward her teepee, and she leant her old body on his arm as they walked.

"Holy mother MaRai, our people will surely die, because my medicine was not powerful enough to hold Skulking Wolf. My heart is indeed troubled. I am in need of your wisdom like never before," whispered Eagle Feather.

"Then my son you must listen well, as this is the last time we'll talk this way. There is much that only the Great Spirit knows and we must trust Wakantanka. You have made your mother proud and our ancestors rest easy. Do not worry. The Crow Nation only wants war so they can capture you and our medicine. There is no other reason, but Skilled as a Fox is too proud to see that. If you were dead there would be no reason to war with our tribe. Beloved son do you wish to die on the battle field with a lance in your chest or to fly like a mighty eagle to our ancestors?" White Feather's questioning smile was pure love.

"I do not fear death, Mother MaRai, I fear to leave you. Who will look after you?" Eagle Feather implored.

"The Great Spirit is enfolding us all in his mighty wings, as you know, and will take care of me and my granddaughter, Dancing Bird. I will tell her of her mighty father and when many moons have passed we shall be together again. Tomorrow as the great Sun touches the mesa, you will fly Eagle Feather and your grandfather White Eagle will be the wind stream beneath your wings."

White Feather kissed his grave face.

"We must prepare ourselves for the dawn."

Eagle Feather rode his horse to the edge of the mesa an hour before dawn and sat astride it searching the horizon for a sign. The air was still and chilly and in the pre-dawn light he offered prayers to the Great Spirit, the Four Directions and thanks to Mother Earth and all her creatures. He thanked his totems and spoke quietly to his horse, the most magnificent one in the herd after the chief's.

"You can be a rascal dear friend, but you are now to carry my daughter Dancing Bird. This night you will carry her where she needs to go."

He backed the horse up to the edge of the cliff and carefully stood on its back facing the canyon, the horse's smooth rump under his feet. The first ray of sunlight was like a laser beam that hit Eagle Feather's face and chest. He opened wide his arms embracing the air and with a deep breath he yelled, "Today I die!" and soared into the rocky canyon two hundred feet below.

A white eagle watched silently from a craggy rock.

Unknown to Skilled as a Fox, at that moment Eagle Feather's mother, Marai White Feather, was sending a smoke signal to the Crow telling them that Eagle Feather was dead and they would find his body in the canyon.

Soon a small band of Crow warriors thundered up to Skilled as a Fox's tepee, dragging the broken body of Eagle Feather and dumped it at the Chief's feet.

"We no longer want to war with you Skilled as a Fox. There is no honour in fighting only women and that seems to be all that is left of your tribe!" The Crow chieftain spat on the ground and galloped away, leaving an enraged Skilled as a Fox and a shocked tribe in their wake.

Eagle Feather's body was taken to his mother's tepee. White Feather tenderly wiped the blood from her dead son's body. He had landed on his feet like a dropping stone and his legs were shattered, the bones sticking through the flesh. Tears of grief poured down her old face as she remembered his willingness to do what she asked.

"You will see, you will see," she crooned as she rocked him with her withered hands, "it will be alright."

After the death of her mother Barren as Hot Sand, Dancing Bird spent much time in the tepee of White Feather, and now she stood at the tent flap, wanting to comfort the old lady and to be comforted, as she too loved Eagle Feather.

"Come in Dancing Bird, I have much to tell you this day." Dancing Bird fell on her knees beside White Feather and they hugged and cried together - Grandmother and Grandaughter of the Eagle.

"We must not waste time child," said White Feather kindly. "Skilled as a Fox is bitterly angry that Eagle Feather robbed him of proving his manhood in battle with the Crow. You must listen carefully as I am getting weak. Skilled as a Fox is not your father. Eagle Feather is your father." She said with great pride swelling her bony chest and then she told Dancing Bird the story of her birth and the reasons for keeping it secret.

"The Crow want our medicine. I am an old woman who will die soon and they do not know of you, so we are safe. Eagle Feather, your father, surrendered his life so that you and the tribe would be spared. His love for us is greater than the great Sun."

Dancing Bird was incredulous.

"Oh Grandmother, I have always loved you both so much. But now I *hate* Skilled as a Fox. He treated my mother badly and now he is responsible for my own true father's death," she sobbed. "Skilled as a Fox has taken away my family. I hate him. I hate him!"

"Shush, little one, shush," White Feather crooned. "The Great Spirit knows what it is doing. Great Grandfather Nanuk tells me that soon the time of the Redman will come to an end. Men with white skin will walk on our beloved Earth mother. They will poison the waters and the air, and kill our animals. They will slaughter even the great whales in the homeland of Nanuk and his totems, seal and polar bear. Whiteskins will make war against the Redman and kill us too, with sticks that shoot fire. They will laugh at our medicine for they do not understand that our gifts are from the Great Spirit and the Great Sun. We must leave our bodies and not walk the Earth at that time. All of us of the Eagle Spirit will watch and wait. Then a time will come after that, when we will again come into bodies, but they will be white skin bodies to teach our medicine to those who are ready. Do not worry little one, we shall all be together again."

"But Grandmother, surely you hate Skilled as a Fox too? Because of him you lost your son," wailed Dancing Bird.

Unperturbed White Feather was slowly mixing a broth in a bowl.

"Ah! When the heart weeps for what is lost, the spirit laughs for what it has found. Skilled as a Fox is your father's blood brother. They shared a great love. Do not forget also, that your father deceived his brother - he was not an innocent. Our Chief has had much to deal with - his own father left him when he was too young - he has learnt much and has great courage. Besides hate is not something that is useful, it blocks our medicine. Drink this broth child and you will be able to release your hate."

Dancing Bird sipped tentatively while her grandmother continued.

"One day the Great Spirit will ask Skilled as a Fox to live as a mother who loses *her* son and he will accept the challenge - only a brave warrior would do that. You see we all eat the flesh from the same carcass. In the eating everyone is nourished and no one is overlooked. The Great Spirit understands all."

"Grandmother White Feather, I'm not sure I understand what you say?" queried the young woman.

"The Great Spirit weaves the Web of Life, child. What is happening now is just one fine thread in it. Yet this thread is connected to all other threads. When we touch part of the Web, the rest of the Web knows." The old woman smiled enigmatically.

"What do you mean 'knows'?" pursued Dancing Bird.

"Two things. The first is that nothing we do goes unnoticed. That every action we take has an affect on everything and everyone else. The second is that all of Life has been woven into the Web. We have all agreed to the weaving. There are no victims my granddaughter and there are, likewise, no heroes, just threads making a picture for the Great Spirit to admire. Never forget that."

White Feather sighed and picking up White Eagle's drum began softly drumming. "Eagle Feather wishes you to have his horse. You have a journey to make this night. He will be with you. Drink up."

The sun was setting when Skilled as a Fox stormed into White Feather's tepee.

"It was *you*, wasn't it? You told my brother to jump?" He glared at White Feather, with nostrils flaring and madness in his eyes. "You stupid old woman. I am Chief and I banish you from our tribe." He grabbed her drum, slashed it with his knife and hurled it onto the ground beside Eagle Feather's body. "You have brought shame to your Chief - GO!"

Dancing Bird screamed for him to be reasonable. He slapped her so hard that she fell to the ground beside the drum.

"You are a cruel and stupid man, I'm so happy that Eagle Feather was my father," she sobbed. Then through her tears she told him the truth of her father.

Blind with anger and humiliation he dragged old White Feather out of the tent and threw her over his horse.

"The Crow wanted Eagle Feather's medicine let's see what they will do with you."

He galloped off into the twilight leaving Dancing Bird still sobbing for her family. Blinded by tears she ran to her father's horse and kicking in frenzy urged the animal at top speed toward the desert where her father, Eagle Feather, was first given to his mother and where that morning he had stepped into the Spirit world. The wind whipped her hair and the horse's sweat was pungent in her nostrils. A sleek cougar, her totem, ran beside. She felt the brush of feathers on each arm as two mighty eagles flew beside her as she rode. Then as if her ride was in slow motion she was transported into the Spirit World and the desert was left far behind. She pulled the horse up at a river and they both drank deeply. The horse whinnied as if sensing a presence. Feeling very alone Dancing Bird whispered hopefully, "Skulking Wolf are *you* here?"

Great Spirit answered, "He is not for you."

The two eagles watched from a crag and a white feather fluttered to her feet. In that instant she knew that White Feather had left her body. Weeping, Dancing Bird lay down on the bank of the river and fell into sound sleep. She heard the drumming of her Grandmother and her spirit followed the beat. A wolf, her father's power animal, led her inside a cave to a deep underground pool. A tortoise, symbolising the creation of Earth... was at her feet where she stood. On the opposite side, the radiant presence of the Great Spirit Wakantanka, glowed with golden-white light. Dancing Bird asked him why he had summoned her.

"You think you are a little dancing bird but really you are a great eagle," he whispered, and with a wave of his hand she was transformed in an instant and flew upward through the roof of the cave. Waiting for her were her soul family – great, great, great grandfather Nanuk, great, great grandfather White Cloud, great grandfather White Eagle, grandmother White Feather and many others. Her father Eagle Feather sat astride his horse and all the totem animals blissfully slept at the family's feet.

"Must I return to the tribe and leave you?" she asked in dismay.

"Not for many, many moons Dancing Bird, and never to leave us. It is time for us all to walk in the spirit world until Wakantanka tells us to walk the Earth again. Then the golden eagle will fly once more and there will come peace.

\*\*\*

Her body, the shell of her soul, was found beside the horse. Dancing Bird's neck was broken. The horse's leg had snapped in a hole and he had stumbled and fallen at high speed.

White Feather's shell was found at the edge of the Crow village.

It's been said that if you hold a shell to your ear, you will hear the sound of the sea;

so I wondered...

What does the shell of a Soul sound like? Perhaps it doesn't have a sound or perhaps the sound of the Soul's shell is in the laughter and the crying - its music - that it has left behind.

Songs and whispers on the winds of time.

Long after the bark has fallen from a tree, the leaves still play in the breeze. Long after the corn has been eaten, the husks still give shelter to tiny insects and beetles. If you listen carefully, you can hear the hidden scrabbling of tiny feet in the corn-soul's shell.

*Could the whisperings from our own psyche also be the music left by another's shell, which we hear as our own? This story shows how that could happen...*

GM

# VERMILLION -THE SWEET EAR AFTER

Reba's face is beautifully dove-like. Her eyes have large dark pupils centered in green and ringed by a black circle. Her high intelligent forehead, round and smooth, has horizontal lines faintly apparent from squinting or perhaps by raising questioning brows. Her hair is straight, long and dark brown.

Reba's nose is small and aquiline, like a dove's beak. Not hooked like a bird of prey, but the tiniest seed-eating beak. Her laugh reveals white even pearls and although her mouth is small, her face still has a generosity of spirit to it. That lovely face is perfectly oval and her chin is chubby. Altogether a dove of peace.

Therein is the truth revealed for Reba has ears bigger than the compassionate one, the Buddha, - huge fleshy, lumbering lobes that catch on her jowls as she bobs her head bird-like up and down, forward and back. Such ears on a woman are almost never seen – almost as big as her palm – but perfectly wonderful. A perfect Picasso on a dove's head. The channels of gristle that define the ears stand out like terraces on a hillside. Not ruddy, or even pink, but a serene cream, with a freckle on the left one. This is not a pedestrian freckle, but a giant splash of cardamom. A magical freckle, on the Buddha's ears, on a dove of peace.

Peace soon to be shattered!

Yesterday Reba found Grace's love letters to Bill. They were hidden between the pages of one of his books and came tumbling out. Feathery, pink-coloured pages that smelt vaguely of incense. Grace was Reba's stepmother but Bill was not her father! Never could she have imagined what 'Pandora's Box' she had opened.

Uncomprehending, Reba stared at the letters on the floor.

Grace had been a wonderful mother to Reba and her sisters and they all grieved unimaginably when she disappeared, but Reba was the one who kept Grace's diary. Reba's father, Douglas, was an Englishman of some stature – physically and financially. He bought a tea plantation in Darjeeling with a business partner, William Desplechin. Douglas was a widower with three small daughters when he met Grace at the Nork-hill Hotel in Gangtok. Of her stay at the Nork-Hill, Grace had written in her diary: *A nursing cat, small in size, short-haired and multi-coloured with milk laden teets swaying, runs past on a mission – stops and inelegantly scratches fleas. How I long for a love child to put to my breast.*

*The sky is not the azure of Australian skies, but softer, with dabs of grey cloud, signaling more rain to*

*come. … into each life some rain must fall…."*

After they were married, Douglas moved them all to London.

Reba thought it odd that Grace had made no mention of her father Douglas in the diary, but many pages *had* been torn out. Grace's diary was the only connection to the mystery of her letters to Bill.

William Desplechin, Bill, as they all called him, had an Australian mother and French father. Bill was a joy. He was boyish, handsome, unpretentious, softly spoken and as gentle as Douglas was severe.

Now even stranger, Reba had discovered Grace's letters to Bill amongst his belongings. She fingered one of the letters trying to fathom the mystery. Before opening them she placed them in order of date stamped on the envelopes and wistfully remembered her stepmother.

For all her apparent contentment, there was a sadness in Grace's grey-green eyes that Reba believed to be a silent longing for Darjeeling – the high mountains shrouded in mists and the ready smiles and kind hearts of the locals. Flattish, Tibet-like faces once embraced Grace as if she were their own. Yet she was not one of them. Her parents were Australian writers who had come to Darjeeling to whet their creative appetites and stayed. All three unable to leave, magnetized by the mystery of the Himalayas.

Now thirty years later Bill had passed away and his belongings, in a huge carved chest, had been sent to Douglas's London estate. Her older sisters had no interest in his stuff, but Reba was nothing like her sisters. The years had not been gentle with Reba. Her mother had died at her birth. She was teased mercilessly because of those ears, yet her failed marriage seemed an even greater disfigurement to her. Now she and her only son were estranged. Loneliness consumed her and she carried wounds that would not heal. Reba longed for true love and had wished that her life had been more like her father's and Grace's. Up until now.

Now she opened the first letter.

*"My One True Beloved Bill,*

*How ecstatic I am that you are still alive, but my darling without you I am dead. It is though I will never breathe again until you hold me close to your heart. Is it karma that we lost each other so cruelly? I would never have married Douglas if I'd known that you survived the 'quake'. He is generous enough, but he is not you. I adore the children – really the main reason why I agreed to marry him – they were so small and with no Mummy – my heart ached for them, especially Rebecca. But not as much as it aches for you my love. And they are not your children – yours and mine - our Aussie heritage – so different from India or cold England.*

*What follows is a copy of my diary entry written in hospital after that ghastly day so many years ago in Darjeeling. The doctor said it would be healing to write my story.*

*I love you. I love you.*

*Journal entry April 19ᵗʰ 1933*

*Everything as it always does, began to heave and change. Not the psychological flexing that Douglas used to manipulate us with, but a real live earthquake.*

*An immediate chill tripped down my arms and I jerked down the sleeves of my green jacket. The only stable thing was the ever-present cloud that hung lazily over the heaving mountains. Before the tremor they hung and now while chaos screamed around the breakfast room, they still just hung – suspended over terror - much like a fixed-eyed idiot at a catastrophe, unable to register alarm or fear.*

*Until that moment, heavenly views, beautiful gentle people and lazy afternoons of lovemaking had marked our sojourn at the New Elgin hotel. That terrible day was the first morning I'd had breakfast without Bill. He was showering and laughing his love for me as I left.*

*The coffee was hot and rich, the omelette slightly tough but still delicious. Thick orange-coloured mango juice added a wicked sweetness.*

*Suddenly and without warning, the floor belched and flung the table upward, spilling my feast over the yellow-checked cloth.*

*My chair lurched sideways and all I could think of was my beloved three floors above me. All around people screamed, fell to the floor and scrambled to their feet, fear making eyes wide and haunted. The mountains shook, while the clouds calm and daydreaming hung and watched our horror.*

*By the time I climbed over the debris of furniture and bodies, a sound had risen from my belly and catapulted from my mouth "Bill! Bill!" I screamed again and again. A broken sound that tore at my ears and my heart. The stairs began to break up before I could reach them – loud cracking shots as wood splintered and snapped and with another belch the mountain hurled most of the hotel into the valley below.*

*My love, you know the rest. How can life be so cruel to those who loved like we did? To discover you are alive after 8 years is a macabre miracle.*

Reba replaced the letter. She was in shock and like a sleepwalker made herself some tea. One drop escaped the spout onto the table.

Being transparent it took on the colour of the red lacquer beneath it. Glistening wet, the size of a pea, it captured Reba. The red made the drop look like blood. She had an urge to tickle the edges with a fingernail to see how far it would draw out. The table paint was hard and shiny, so she expected it would stretch a long way. Certainly further than on balsa wood, which would have drank it by now. Yet there it sat boldly defiant of evaporation or thirsty wood. Reba wondered how long she would be able to leave it alone. She understood defiance - the girl who wore her ears as a defiant badge against a hostile world. How could she guess where that badge was about to take her?

Instead of tampering with the droplet, Reba dressed for dinner and slipped another of Grace's letters to Bill into her purse.

*****

Giovani, the owner of *Amore Bello,* showed Reba to her favourite corner in his restaurant. Something passed between them – an unexplored romantic fragrance? Reba ordered and ate while she read Grace's familiar scrawl expressing her undying love for Bill, as well as her loathing of Calcutta. Reba smiled and nodded to herself as she read, as she too hated the place. Giovani watched and also smiled.

*"Most beloved friend and love of my life Bill,*

*Wednesday, 17ʰ May 1947 - we've been here in Calcutta for three days. I miss you more than ever and love you deeper than you can ever know. I wish I could show you. We must find a way to be together when this trip with the family is over.*

*Calcutta is a jangling juxtaposition of elegance and effluence. Sons and daughters of the dark mother Kali. Well may she poke out her tongue in disgust! Her ever-generating children overwhelm her – a calamity of humanity. Kali's mosaic'd temple is even eclipsed by her bustling brood. Brisk walking Bengalis, fast talking traders, endless comings and goings, amid timeless being. Buses, bikes and taxis jerking, scooting and hooting in organised chaos. Incessant honking, yet all moving in uncanny synchronicity. Men spit and urinate in every street. Dogs, men and babies lie corpse-like in the midday heat – oh! the oppressive heat. Thick and humid air, sucks sweat from our bodies, then leaves us to squelch in our wetness.*

*The Oberoi Grand Hotel where we shall stay 'till departure is a blatant colonial absurdity amid crushing squalor – an oasis of beauty and composure in Kali's magnificent ugliness. Elegance infused with an all-pervading pong. The odour seeps into every pore of every thing. Tincture of humanity, with fumes and smoke, plus a dash of incense. Altogether more repugnant by the hour.*

*If you were here it would immediately become paradise.*
*Forever Yours Alone*
*Grace."*

Later Reba laid a hand on Giovani's as she paid the bill. "Thankyou," she smiled deep into his brown eyes.

"I'll see you again soon." Giovani said and watched her leave with fast-beating heart.

\*\*\*

The discovery of Grace and Bill's romance had made Reba more introspective than usual. *This bedside chest is as boring as – I was going to say beeswax, but beeswax can be anything but boring.* Reba sat on her bed and mused.

*Nice enough box but the chips of missing wood annoy the hell out of me. My daughter-in-law was given to throwing things at my son in frustration – who could blame her, he's so like his grandfather. Now this chest is mine and I have to hide the chips under books and tissue boxes. Blast them! One day I'll have one of my own which smells of camphor wood and has no signs of warfare. Meanwhile this will do. I must have a home for my beautiful emerald-green silk glasses case, embroidered with an elaborate ostrich feather – the turquoise and lime green stitching is magical, as if by chance lifted from the silk it would float in the air like a real feather. My reading glasses slip so sensuously into the silky softness every night to sleep beside me. Oh! god, could a man fall in love with me just from looking at my bedside box? My books of poetry, philosophers ancient and modern, and teachers from around the world, would tell him I'm a student of humanity, which must surely interest any worthwhile male. And my glasses case – how could he not see the artiste', the eye for beauty and colour in me…greens and blues and purples – more divine than the dramatic and warring reds and oranges. Gentle, receptive passionate purple – not lustful like the hot colours!* Reba smiled. *Although if he wanted more fire, perhaps I could say I made those ugly chips. Yes! I could say I was frustrated because a former lover wouldn't accommodate my wicked lust. So I hit the box again and again!* She laughed out loud at her own nonsense. *Perhaps I could just fill the chips with beeswax and he could love me anyway?*

Devoid of excuses to continue her daydreaming, Reba stared then at the heavy chest on her floor. Stained dark and decoratively carved, it smacked of Islander art. All of Bill's possessions were inside and now Reba began rifling through them – her mission to find something that would explain Grace's mysterious disappearance. An ornate brown leather cover caught Reba by surprise. The last page was not only surprising, but also shocking. In Bill's neat script she read…

*4th July 1951*
*"It is the saddest night for I am leaving and not coming back. Anguish, dreadful anguish. Mountains rise dark and dangerous from the sea floor. Captain calls time to pull anchor. How can I leave my beloved's bones on this evil island? The pain in her eyes drove me almost insane before she slipped away. Oh Grace, my angel Grace how can I go on without you?"*

*"Go," she whispered on the wind. My bones stay, but I come with you my love. It's all right.*

*It's all right."*

Reba clasped a shaking hand to her mouth, then made a phone call to a clairvoyant.

"10.30 tomorrow morning it is then," she said.

***

The fortune-teller had answered some of Reba's questions regarding Bill and Grace, and now Reba wanted to know her own future.

"According to your destiny, you've had many harrowing moments Reba."

"What the hell do you mean by harrowing Simon?" She quizzed accompanied by a nervous laugh.

Simon-the-Wise led Reba into the nuances of harrowing. He told her that everyone experiences words uniquely, according to their individually coloured 'lens'.

"What is your favourite colour Reba?"

"Vermillion, I suppose – in this moment," she said without absolute conviction, and added, "It's the colour of joy and happiness somehow."

A knowing smile flicked across Simon's face.

"And what else is it?"

Reba pursed her lips before quoting Teilhard de Chardin, *'Some day, after we have mastered the winds, the waves, the tides and gravity, we shall harness the energies of love. Then for the second time in the history of the world, man will have discovered fire.'* Then she surprised herself, declaring adamantly, "Vermillion is fire!"

"And what is your least favourite colour Reba?"

She sat fully upright, remembering Bill's journal.

"Brown – yes definitely brown!"

Simon-the-Wise led her along a psychological path to her own knowing, by exclaiming that 'harrowing' for her was coloured brown.

Feigning ignorance Reba asked Simon what he meant. So he asked Reba to describe brown. "How does it smell and taste? What songs does it sing? How does it feel? Does brown dance slowly or fast, light or heavy, happy or sad?"

She rested her head on one hand tilting to the right; the freckle on her left ear winked in the candle -light.

"Mmm – brown – brown – we-e-ll – it smells disgusting like dogs manure and tastes even worse. Brown doesn't sing songs at all Simon! Ever! Brown dances with leaden feet, slow, clumping, like a funeral procession – the coffin is heavy, so heavy that the bearers struggle with every step. Brown, mmm? How does it feel? I need to really think about that."

"Don't *think* Reba, get out of your head – *feel* it – *feel* the brown – really feel the brown!

Reba began to cry. "It feels empty somehow." Slow gentle sobs released rivers of tears, which she caught with a tissue before they dripped wet and salty onto her ample bosom. Simon was all compassion.

"Cry Reba, let your grief out".

And Reba cried. She cried for her dead mother, for an unloving father, for her dead Gracie, for her ex-husband and for her son. She sobbed and shook while Simon held her and encouraged her.

"Let all that black out dear lady, let it out, let it out," he murmured. "You have finally acknowledged your life m'dear and although there is one more harrowing moment, your future is rosy red."

Reba swallowed loudly, her ears doing their thing.

"How can you be so sure?" she asked.

"You yourself have told us both. Vermillion is the colour of the heart, the colour of joy and happiness…the colour of fire …and LOVE! Very soon you will know what I'm talking about. Brown is nothing more than vermillion with a little black added. Black is love lost. Your emptiness – the blackness - will soon be all gone – and only vermillion will remain."

Reba stood to leave. Simon's eyes twinkled as he stared into the ether.

"Grace wants you to know that she goes with you. She says' it is all right, it is all right'."

The last words in Bill's journal flashed in her memory. '*I come with you my love. It's all right, it's all right.*'

"Oh God!" Was all Reba could manage as tears blinded her way home.

***

In denial of her lusty lobes, Reba wore dangling beaded earrings of enormous proportions, to dine at Giovani's that night.

Meal over, she pushed back her chair to leave. Reba's skirt, her favourite black one with the embroidered peacocks, caught under a steel leg. She rose at the same time tripping and falling against the wall. Every dining eye was upon her now. She tried to regain her balance, but the earring on her left ear snagged on the wall light. The brass bracket held fast to the gold of the earring as she fell. Everyone held their breath expecting the ear to be ripped from the beautiful pigeon head. But no! The ear stretched and stretched like some mysterious rubber. Her backside bounced off the small oval table beneath the lamp while her ear hung like meat on a butcher's hook.

Reba was fully upright again in an instant. With an elegance born of practice she deftly released the earring from the brass claws, straightened her clothes and smoothed down her soft hair. Swiping an index finger under her tiny beak, she glided past the other diners seemingly oblivious to their stares.

"Brown, harrowing bloody brown," she chanted to herself and left Giovani's, while behind her the entire restaurant gasped.

It was only after she was well clear of the restaurant, that she dared take a hand to the ear and allow those beautiful eyes to leak hot tears of humiliation that seared her flushed cheeks. A splotch of blood on her fingers explained the pain and seemed punishment somehow for her deformity.

"Hardly Vermillion?" she snorted.

Giovani had watched her the whole time, holding back his

desperate need to assist her for fear of humiliating her further. Transfixed, he mused about her visits to his restaurant.

*At first I didn't notice her ears. But as we became more familiar I thought they were larger than one so beautiful should endure. Her face is so pretty and her voice is pretty too. She asked me to 'please call me Reba instead of M'am.' I told her it was an unusual name and she said it was short for Rebecca. At school she was called Becky – Pecky-Becky - and she hated it, so she gave herself Reba. She is an artist and sits for hours sketching in her favourite alcove sipping my coffee. I love to see her mysterious eyes looking at me over the cup. Oh! those eyes. This evening is a nightmare for us both. I want to follow her into the street, to comfort her, to kiss her ear – but then everyone would know how I have come to love her. But what an agony if she never comes back! This is an unbearable thought. All around my customers are laughing loudly at a clumsy woman with big ears and gaudy earrings. Bastards! Bastards! I must go to her.* Giovani lurched into the dark street; his mind racing like greyhounds.

*The street is shiny – hmmm shower of rain, but it's dark and empty. Thank God, a taxi waiting with the motor running.*

Giovani found himself blubbering to the driver as he fell in the cab door. "Quickly, quickly, I'm looking for a woman. This way! This way!" He pointed down the street where he had often watched her walk; now empty of his Reba. The cab cruised down the street, while he scanned the footpaths. He didn't know where she lived or how far away. Upstairs or downstairs? Street level or basement? Panic rose in his throat as if he were being choked. Then there she was, flagging down *his* taxi.

God in heaven, thankyou, he silently prayed. Reba slipped into the back seat, quietly and uneasily. Giovani turned around from the front seat, to see the outline of his angel holding one delicate hand to her left ear.

"Reba it is I, Giovani. Please let me take you home?"

Reba was startled to find the taxi occupied. She blinked in the gloom, her mind flying. *I should have recognised that smell,'* she thought. *'Giovani's immediate attraction for me was his cologne – even more than his delicious aromatic pasta dishes. He isn't tall – I don't like tall men – and although he is a little thick around his middle, I couldn't say fat. Sometimes his forearm extends from his shirt as he lays a dish on the table and a sigh escapes me. His skin is so soft looking and such a golden cinnamon colour that I often have to touch it. "Thanks Giovani, that looks amazing," I say, indicating the food, but meaning his arm.*

Longing to know what she was thinking, Giovani waited patiently as he held Reba's gaze. However Reba was lost in her memories.

*I often walk home wondering how it would feel to have both of those magnificent arms around me. His hair is graying at the temples, but his face is empty of wrinkles. He could be 45 or 70 I don't care. I love him, dream of him, even hunger for him in my lonely hours. His deep brown eyes have hidden depths and when he looks at me my stomach lurches. Now he asks to take me home and I, the humiliated one don't feel worthy of such care.*

In the damp darkness of a London night, Grace whispered, *"It's all right Reba. It's all right,"* and Reba gasped aloud.

Giovani could wait no longer and blurted, "I love you Reba! I love you! I love you!" And in a heartbeat Reba's world turned from brown to vermillion.

\*\*\*

Speaking too loudly, Brigadier Brown put aside the book he was reading and regaled his fellow club members in pompous style.

"There was this bloody woman in the restaurant last night. In truth I would never have noticed her unless she'd had that fall; given as I am to keeping my own company and counsel, unlike so many other nosy people. I really only lifted my head from my lasagna when the god-awful commotion started. I don't usually note peculiarities about others – nothing to do with me. But by God, the ears on that woman – massive bits of bloody meat that the foolish tart had decorated with equally massive bloody earrings!

Surely she'd know that to <u>hide</u> a defect is more socially acceptable. I mean to say – when she tripped and fell, I would have thought 'serves you right' if I was that sort of chap, but then one of those hideous bits of junk jewelry caught on a brass wall light and nearly ripped her bloody ear right orrf. Sounds like I'm a connoisseur of gaudy jewelry, which of course I have no interest in – anyway she managed to right herself again and left the restaurant, but by God it was in an uproar. I of course paid little attention, while all around me others made derogatory comments – rather rude and unkind I reckon. Still one has to wonder why the silly cow would not have surgery or at least hide those monstrous lugs under a hat. Nothing to do with me though. By God, I was moved to write a little poem about those ears, but I'm no poet and I'm certainly not equipped to comment on another's defect, having no discernible ones m'self – damned fortunate wouldn't you say? Anyway I had a nice lager and scribbled this – ready chaps, listen 'ere…

Diners stare
Ears so rare
Silly mare
Elephant ears
All her fears
End in tears
Brigadier cheers
Orders beers
To celebrate
Rightness!"

Brigadier Brown guffawed at his own wit then reached for his book. "Jolly interesting book I'm reading chaps – 'Vermillion' by William Desplechin – it's about cannibalism on an island in the Pacific – poor chap's wife, Grace, bloodywell got eaten."

***

On a bed, beside a box that was boring as beeswax, Reba laid her head on Giovani's shoulder and said that brown truly can lose its black and become vermillion.

"You are so right," he said.

*Some people have difficulty believing that we drop and pick up bodies as we move through lifetimes. Yet new, fresh cells become old withered cells and we must leave.*

*Every ending heralds a new beginning -*
*somehow, someway...*

*We all understand that, irrespective of what journeys we believe lay ahead...*

*Yet so many of us cling to our bitter thoughts, wanting another to rescue us from tedium...*

*waiting for romantic love to ignite our self-love...and love of LIFE.*

*LIVE spelled backward is EVIL.*
*So I wondered...*

*what would it take to wake us up to our creative, expectant self -*
*to make us want to LIVE instead?*
*An unexpected death perhaps...*

*GM*

# CAESAR'S QUIETUS

The day we buried Cleo was cold as Julys are; dry and starkly bright so that I wore sunglasses, which was a deliverance because I didn't want my anguish to be seen. I say *we* buried Cleo, but really I dug the hole near the grevillias, while he just held the feather with which we would mark her grave.

***

I'd been killing time tending these botanical gardens since retiring from Academia. Cleo had appeared in my garden like a starburst on a black sky and captured me in a heartbeat.

"You look like a philosopher," she grinned as I pushed the barrow past her.

"Very perceptive young lady!" Despite the call of the compost heap, I stopped the barrow and dug my hands into my overalls like a schoolboy. For me to be acknowledged for one's brain was very seductive. Yet I could never have imagined how seductive Cleo was to become to me.

I puffed out my chest like the tiny finches on a branch above our heads.

"I was a Professor of Philosophy in another life," I told her.

"Well as I am truly in the presence of greatness, would I be a total nuisance to talk to you from time to time?" Cleo was serious, although her twinkling eyes offered me something in return. Unashamedly ego-stroked, I was lassoed by her from that second. All I could do was grin like a fool and mumble something about it being a highlight of my day to talk to her.

"I'm Cleo." She held out her hand and I noticed how weathered it was. Her handshake was genuinely warm while she dismissed my apology of garden dirt with a compliment.

"Anyone who loves plants makes my heart sing; and no Cleo isn't short for Cleopatra." She smiled and a dimple in her cheek winked. I laughed, throwing back my head to the blue sky.

"Well Cleo, I'm Julius, no joke m'dear. Julius and not-Cleopatra eh?"

"Hail Caesar!" she giggled; then seriously said, "How old are you, can I ask?"

She would always have a way of bringing me back to the moment. I told her that I would tell her if she would tell me, hoping that, like a lot of women she would decline.

"I'm fifty six." Her face showed she wasn't sure if it was a good thing or not.

Cleo looked unbelievably younger than that and I was relieved that the gap in our ages was less than I thought. "I'm an old bloke Cleo – seventy four now."

We stared at each other smiling; scanning the other's life, wondering.

Cleo graced the garden often, always staying only briefly. She was a yoga teacher who had been a dancer and still walked with perfect posture. There was a childlike quality about her despite her extraordinary knowledge of so many things.

"I must do a cartwheel on your beautiful green grass Julius," she'd laugh and amaze me with her agility. It was not only this that amazed me, but her intellect.

"I brought you some brazil nuts darling," she'd say showing her mothering side. "You need to eat about six a day to get enough selenium!" Then she'd bounce into a lecture on the importance of selenium for balancing brain chemistry. She wanted to save the world from the epidemic of depression. I just wanted her to save me. Perhaps one day I might tell Cleo about the backstabbing at the university and my subsequent breakdown. Now it was enough that she had revived my flagging spirit and tantalized my tired brain with little notes that she would give me as she ran off; a peck on the cheek and her perfume all that lingered.

*"The gift in all experience is knowledge.*
*The gift in knowledge is wisdom.*
*In wisdom is strength. Go there Caesar.*
*Holding you close,*
*but not so close that you can't fly like an eagle.*
*Love from Cleo."*

That night as she 'held me close' I cleared the detritus off my piano and fingered old memories; the first time in twenty years that I'd wanted to make music.

At times I'd stumble upon Cleo engrossed in writing and felt excluded.

"I didn't know you were in the gardens," I'd say with disapproval in my voice, as though she must seek me out. Like I began to seek her. I'd lie in bed at night and read and re-read every single word she wrote, searching for deeper, hidden meanings. I had fallen in love and I wanted her to be in love with me. Yet she was always running off. Her diary is so full she told me. Cleo got sucked into everyone's pitiful melodramas. She saw them as birds with broken wings that needed splinting! Sometimes she would be minding grandchildren or the most painful admission of all – "I'm meeting my lovely husband for coffee."

I wished that she were meeting *me* for coffee. In some atmospheric little coffee bar, filled with artists and philosophers – *our* sort of people.

***

Now while I dug, her husband stood, grim-faced and uncomprehending. I didn't pity him. Didn't he have her while I hungered for any crumbs she might throw to me? Cleo was a tiny thing and incongruously her husband was a big man. She was much better suited to *me*. When she gave me her warm goodbye hugs our bodies had fitted together better than him and her, surely?

***

"Bring me some more of your poetry Cleo," I'd smile at her, surreptitiously offering myself as a subject for her flights of fancy. Pruning and trimming now became a time for perfecting my fantasy. Her poetry would surely cast me as her hero. Gone the pain in my arthritic fingers. Each squeeze of the secateurs made my pulse race and I'd catch myself grinning broadly; a simpleton of sorts; but I didn't care. I was besotted.

"This is something I wrote twenty years ago." Cleo handed me a sheet, flushed and breathless. "I've got to go Julius, I must write while I have some time."

Dashed, I sat on a bench and read. And read again.

*MY HEART*
*Days of brooding silences*
*Thoughts on wings*
*Nights of restless longing*
*Sleepless*
*Dreaming*
*Longing, wanting.*
*Mornings wet with dew and tears*
*And you*
*Not here*
*Away*
*I have to face another day*
*Without you.*
*Darkness comes to blanket me*
*Alone I cry and then*
*Daylight to break*
*My heart again*

How could she have written so poignantly about my *own* emptiness? Perhaps this is really for *me*? Did she want to be with me as much as I want to be with her? Somewhat disoriented, I swallowed painkillers for my aching back.

The next day everything changed.

Cleo said her husband was taking her to India on a 'Writer's Retreat'. She'd write to me. She did, just one letter.

*Dearest Julius,*

*My husband was right to believe that India would inspire the writer in me! We are in Calcutta temporarily before going to Darjeeling. The heat is killing! The Traders are even more stifling than the weather. The stench of sewerage flowing over the footpaths is rather disconcerting and I can't wait to breathe the air of the Himalayas. People seem so desperately poor it breaks my heart. I keep giving away our money to beggars.*

*I long for your cool, green gardens and wonder how many of these souls actually live before they die? Do we?*

*Amazing to think Calcutta has spawned Ramakrishna and Yogananda. If only you and your gardens were here.*

*Be well and be all that you can be!*
*Love and care*

*Cleo*

I didn't give a rat's about India or Ramakrishna! Time dragged and it was all I could do to cry an old man's tears of frustration and read her words. *"If only you were here."* Months passed and I had her in an ashram somewhere with some bloody guru, old Julius forgotten.

An eternity later she walked across the lawn to where I was weeding the grevillia bed. We hugged and she said I looked well. Then she stroked the leaves of the grevillia and said she missed them and all the birds that came to suck their nectar. I needed her to say she missed *me!*

"I haven't been back here for so long Prof, because I have found my calling and I'm like a woman possessed." Her excitement was palpable and I was so relieved to see her again, that I somehow missed the implication of her words. Cleo handed me more of her poetry. "This will explain why I can't come to the gardens anymore. I hope you will understand."

Feeling suddenly inconsequential I was left holding more of Cleo's words, but not her.

### KILLING TIME?
*A soul is born*
*Tick tock*
*Flesh inhabited.*
*Just once.*
*This time.*
*Seconds and seconds of time.*
*Tick tock*
*Flesh ravaged by a ravenous time.*
*Time too short to find heaven in the hell.*
*Sucking at the breast of dogmas*
*Blind to their own miracle*
*They say*
*I gave my body for love.*
*I sold my soul for wealth.*
*I traded my self for reward.*
*And the excuse of cowards,*
*I was a victim.*
*Remorsefully as they are gobbled up*
*Every banal second, tick tock*
*Given to another,*
*Every tired, disillusioned second*
*Spent as a sacrifice to beliefs*

*Tick tock*
*Or in apology to oneself;*
*Excuses that steal power*
*Tick tock*
*Is a second lost forever,*
*Deducted from one's life.*
*One's creative life.*
*Therein is the hell.*

*Stop the clock!*

*Heaven is the texture of colours*
*Slippery paint on fingers.*
*Cadence of notes. Words on paper.*
*Or tongue. Sung with every throbbing cell.*
*Stone or wood re-modelled. Earth reformed.*
*Rhythmic feet, skipping, jumping, flying.*

*Love, wealth, reward*
*Belongs to the creating soul.*
*Tick.*

I hated her 'tick tocks' all through the piece as if I were clock-watching on death row! I loathed her reference to decaying flesh. Yes, I had traded my integrity for reward! Yes, I had sold my soul for love and for what? I detested myself for feeling like a victim, but that is what I am damn it! 'Killing Time' she called it – couldn't she see that this was killing me? Perhaps I misinterpreted though. Perhaps she would return tomorrow and say, "Caesar it is time for you and I to create together". Surely that is it. Yes, surely that's it.

The next day, while every joint in my body yelped with crippling arthritis, Cleo did return, but not to create.

"I remember reading about a famous pianist", she said, "who was so crippled with arthritis he could hardly walk or move his fingers yet when he walked to the piano he walked with a spring in his step and his fingers became fluid. It's not too late to find *your* calling Julius." She placed her hand on my cheek and told me she was 'feeling' my pain. I winced. I couldn't stand her smugness. I thought I *had* found my purpose. *She* was my purpose and now I wanted her to feel the loss that I was feeling. I was scathing of her poetry; almost insulting but I couldn't stop.

"Did you think putting the 'tick tocks' in smaller print would stop them jarring and distracting the reader? Well it didn't work!" I was shaking and sounded hysterical even to myself. When she placed her hand on my arm I wrenched it away like a petulant child.

"You could have another twenty five years of life Julius. Please don't waste yourself by just killing time," she said intently. Cleo placed a letter in the barrow and walked out of my life with a whispered, "Carpe diem Caesar".

Seize the day? Seize the day! I was 74 years old. My days were numbered!

*Dearest Julius*

*My one wish for you is to find the source of joy within yourself.*

*This is how I describe finding my calling and know that you will relate - when I'm in 'that place' my physicality disappears; pain and tiredness simply evaporate.*

*My spirit is soaring like I've never experienced and every cell in my body feels alive in ways that are similar to falling in love. A door has opened and a whole world of wonder is flying out. I suspect that creativity is the natural state for us all and however we express it is perfect - provided our heart beats faster when we think of it, our eyes glow in anticipation of doing it and even before the thing is done, we are designing the next 'love child'.*

*This is Plato's Eros I suspect.*

*How and why I waited so long to surrender to this is beyond me. Please, please find joy in your music again. The clock is ticking dear friend. Don't waste a second. Goodbye dear Julius. I'll never forget you.*

"Fuck you Cleo!" I screamed gouging the tears from my face.

***

Her husband watched me as I emptied Cleo's ashes into the hole that I'd numbly dug with aching hands. "Cleo knew it wasn't actually legal to bury her ashes in a botanical garden, but she said that you would do it for her." His voice was flat.

"How could she know that I wonder?" I said aloud, but more to myself.

"She was psychic," the husband said matter-of-factly. "This is an eagle feather to mark the spot. Cleo said it was to remind you to …er…fly like an eagle."

I hardened even more, thinking eagles don't fly with broken wings.

"Thanks mate," he said softly and walked away. I didn't get up, just knelt there; empty as the urn he carried. Then he was back holding out an envelope. "I'm Antony, by the way. Cleo wanted you to have a copy of this."

The pain in my body was as unbearable as my loss. I fell back next to Cleo's remains.

Bark-chips dug into me through my shirt as I read her poem in the July glare.

## HOLOGRAPHIC US

*Imagine yourself psychic.*

*Go on imagine.*
*Now walk confidently upon my landscape.*
*Drenched with the colours that I paint.*
*Under your toes feel the grit of my path*
*And with certainty know where it leads.*
*A junction? Left or right, forward or back;*

*Follow with expectation*
*Of a glorious find.*

*A wall you find instead?*
*Don't turn back*
*It may be illusion*
*Your own self projected.*
*Or a shy smoke screen to test your mettle.*
*Your psychic self is unperturbed.*
*Merge your Merlin-mind with the blockage;*
*Stride through, soar over, burrow underneath*
*Shape-shift to the other side.*
*Then triumphantly sniff the perfume of understanding.*
*Finger the textures of knowing*
    *Snack on morsels of possibility.*
*Whisperings from another's soul.*
*Yet the sound of yourself.*
*Your own image reflected in my glass.*
*How can that be?*

*We are as one.*

### From Cleo

With closed eyes I smiled wryly and remembered W.H.Auden's words.

*If we really want to live, we'd better start at once to try; if we don't it doesn't matter, we'd better start to die.*

Et tu Brutus?

Cleo said "Heaven is the texture of colours." Ningrapo's grandfather waited beyond the rainbow. Is that where Heaven is?

Others say there's
a pot of gold
at the end of a rainbow;

so I wondered...
if rays of coloured light could transport a person to places unimaginable?

What does a colour mean?

What if the pot of gold was found inside a heart and soul and not at a certain place; would that mean that the rainbows are inside us waiting to be revealed?

And if that is true, what must we do to reveal the rainbows?
This is a story that tells how.

GM

# THE OMEGA CHRONICLES

*Part 1*

Lymei's bony head was on the ground. My father Wedran was in the graveyard; shovel in hand, soft brown earth all around. Lymei's coffin had long disappeared but the huge rusty nails that held it together were in a pile off to the side. Father placed the nails carefully around the skull, like numbers on a sundial, and then stood back to admire his work. The light of the full moon made it look like a macabre mandala. He noticed me then.

"Narbiah," he softly acknowledged my presence.

"Father." I bowed my head slightly.

"You're just in time. Lymei will be glad you are here." I detected a slight thrill to his usual calm, deep voice. "Did you bring the crystals?"

"I have them all Father. Here." The leather bag was heavy in my hand.

"Do you remember the placement?" He raised an eyebrow, which distorted the tattoo on his forehead. I was again relieved that my tattoo was hidden under hair at the nape of my neck.

"I'll try Father, but it's been many years since great- grandmother Lymei showed me. I was only nine Earth years I think."

Even with the full moon it was difficult to identify the individual crystals, so I used my inner vision.

"The emerald at the third eye; ruby in the left eye and amber in the right? Diamond in the mouth; but what of these two?" I showed him a black onyx and a blue sapphire on my open palm.

"You've done well Narbiah. Those are for the ears. Did you bring the Accelerator from the vault?"

"Oh no! I forgot!" What would you have me do? Will it be too late if I go now?"

My father was a just man. He believed consequences of actions were the best teachers. However this was far too important to wait for consequences to catch up with me. He laughed and his teeth flashed white in the darkness.

"Narbiah I knew you'd forget."

He threw the Accelerator to me and I fell backwards to catch it, grinning like a clown. Father checked his timepiece and the position of Orion and Venus with the Moon.

"We've got time for drink – anything you fancy?"

"Something for forgetfulness seems appropriate," I chuckled.

Father made the brews from his stash of herbs he'd compressed into cubes. He would occasionally drop them into a friend's soup to charge an atmosphere. I loved his mischievousness.

"What's this?" I took the steaming mug from him.

"A love potion," he said matter-of-factly.

"A love potion!" I yelled incredulously. "We are about to make a shift to the Omega dimension. What if the life forms there are dead-ugly and I get a crush on one?"

Both eyebrows were raised this time. "Should be highly amusing I reckon. Drink up Kiddo, it's getting cold."

With the Accelerator in one hand, I sipped the hot liquid with the other - both a profound experience. Then Wedran's inner eye fell on the message stick in my pocket.

"So what's this, then?" His eyebrows made the tattoo dance.

"Knowing that I would not be returning *ever* to the planet called Earth I thought it wise to leave behind some information. If someone finds my chronicles, then their time is also getting close. I only wish to serve, Father." I said.

He stood up and stretched his nine hundred year old body, then bent down to touch my forehead.

His thumbprint was hot over my third eye.

"I see the potion is working already sweet Narbiah. It is a good thing that you do."

He asked for the message stick and without hesitation I held it out to him, knowing he could scan it for anything not worthy to leave. My inner vision scanned my chronicles along with his.

*The history of our family was long. We carry the keys of the Hue Menn. It was always a bone of contention for me that people of Earth, in their forgetfulness, called the species 'hu<u>man</u>' and the males of the species <u>men</u>! As though only the males, held the keys. Those two millennia* *were dark indeed. Yet you are perhaps wondering why I call you, the reader a Hue Mann.*

*You, the reader of these chronicles, are a member of a family of souls that number one hundred and forty four thousand – sometimes called a monad. We came to Earth when it was time to leave the last dimension. You are familiar with seven colours, yes? But from the seven primary colours are derived one hundred and forty four thousand hues. Thus you - and I once - were called a Hue Mann. That term was locked into the collective consciousness over millennia, and it was soon translated into 'human'. The term man or woman is a bastardization of information and served the purpose of patriarchal dominance. Throughout Earth's <u>recorded</u> history (his story) as designated by the same order of masculine dominant Hue Menn, the illusion of duality has been perpetrated by this his/her, man/woman paradigm.*

*The number of souls that express the Divine Dream are what Earthlings or Hue Menn know as Avogaddro's number – an almost unimaginable number $6.0221415 \times 10$ to $23^{rd}$ – all divided into families or pods of 144,000 members. While existing on and in the Earth dimension, the families are called Hue Menn to distinguish them from other dimensional families, such as the Suna Me in the eighth dimension. The Suna Me are almost indistinguishable from ourselves.*

Wedran, my beloved Father, wise teacher and friend walked slowly around Lymei's mandala, my message stick held in his bony hand. He nodded often as he read, but never once met my gaze; both of us lost in the scanning of my chronicles.

*"The Divine Dreamer fragmented itself into the cosmos to experience its own creation. Much like you as a sleeping Earthling has dreams, which are created by your consciousness, so the Divine Dreamer, dreams its creation too. Earth soul families will live many 'dreams', each time refining its consciousness, until it merges again with the Divine Consciousness. The Earth plane is one dimension in thirty-three through which a soul family or pod will travel.*

*Families of Hues cannot permanently leave this dimension until every member has attained liberation from desires. Even desiring liberation is a desire of itself. This dimension is ruled by desires and has very thick dense energy. It is difficult to free one's consciousness from such a magnet. But it can be done and one day (or night) exactly as my father and I are about to do, you also will be ready for the next dimension. Once there you will again meet with other family members who have prepared the way for you.*

*Soul families share the same consciousness and meet again and again through many incarnations to facilitate the opening of the Divine Eye in every member.*

*What I share next is very relevant information for you. It is guaranteed to make your sojourn on this dense plane easier.*

My father's measured tread came to a halt.

"Guaranteed Narbiah? Guaranteed? Going to give them their investment back if it's not true?" He twinkled.

I blushed. "I can hardly believe I said that." I offered. "In truth I can only say that it helped make <u>my</u> passage easier".

Wedran nodded. "Good, good – whatever the Dreamer is creating we must trust that what you are leaving is designed. Ah! Sweet mystery."

I so loved him. He continued with his pacing around the portal to Omega that we would soon create. Again we met at our inner vision to continue reading my chronicles.

*"If this message stick is in your hands, then I know you are open to receive this vital information. Many Hue Menn will find this too hard to accept and will take much longer than yourself to achieve 'lift off'."*

"Lift-off? Interesting choice of words my girl." A grin split my father's face. "You have always made me laugh. Do you remember our incarnation and subsequent guillotining during the French Revolution of the 1600's? During all the fear and drama you told the executioner that everyone could see his penis and he should hide it because it was so small. It stalled him for a moment. But what a moment! Now where were we?"

I snickered.

*There are seven steps to your liberation. One - be one with the Earth. Two - master your emotions. Three - know your own power. Four - open your heart. Five - speak your truth. Six - look beyond the veil. Seven - become the lucid dreamer.*

*Other dimensions will have a different number of steps, but you can experience seven colours, and each one holds a key. Allow me to explain the steps using the colours. Heed them carefully.*

Father nodded in approval.

*Red – all experiences, yes ALL, even supposedly drastic and painful ones, are manifested by you. Every single one, even tiny insignificant ones contain a gift. Never doubt it. You choose to position yourself in the Divine Dream to attain the gift. If you loose sight of the gift, it was a wasted experience and you will need to repeat it. Many of us have to repeat a Dreaming many times before we 'wake up'. You have your roots in the mother Earth and the colour red is the vibration of the root energy center in the body. Therefore be like the mother Earth - be one with the Earth. Accept and continue to re-generate. Trees grow from seed without anguish. Flowers bloom without fear. Rivers flow to their origins – the great oceans - naturally. Prey accepts their fate, knowing that life is born of death. An event can only happen to you with your consent. If it is happening, then you have agreed. Therefore rejoice; do not complain!*

*Orange – Hue Man's emotion is the energy that judges. Judgment of good, bad, right, and wrong, is born of strong emotion. Even great ecstasy is an emotion capable of holding you back in your quest for liberation. Strong emotions lead Hue Menn into many circumstances where the energy is so dense it is like glue that keeps them stuck. The colour orange is also aligned with the sexual energy center in the body and strong emotions can lead Earthlings into unnatural and deviant acts that bind them to the body rather than to the soul. Some teachers of religion use high emotion, reward and punishment, to bind their followers to a particular belief. This is imprisoning instead of liberating and is also glue-like energy. Again be like the mother Earth, balanced in all things. Distance yourself from emotion and you won't get stuck like a fly in web. Practice acceptance of everything and you will move quickly forward. Acceptance is a great liberator.*

*Yellow – Hue Menn struggle for power without realizing they have great power to ordain their fate. This point is the key that will unlock within you a reservoir of creativity. If you truly knew that you were intrinsically powerful, you would without doubt create a life of joy and happiness. If that is not the current blueprint of your life, then by definition you do not know your own power. The colour yellow is at the center of your body at your solar plexus and like the Sun that gives this planetary solar system life, powering it with heat and light, so the sun at your center will do that for you also, once you accept it. Know your own power and then the door of wisdom will open to you.*

*Green – When you can fully open your heart, without fear or favour, the speed of your potential for liberation increases exponentially. The colour green is the energy vibration of your heart center. When Hue Menn speak of love, they confuse Divine Love with an emotional need to be with another. They speak of their heart's desire or of getting a broken heart. Then more confusion comes - is it love or lust? Is it love or security? Is it love or friendship? The heart center opens and closes like a door in the wind. To truly open your heart you first must experience your own acceptance and your own power - without emotion. Listen to the wisdom of the heart, not the head. Then the opening will happen naturally and you will feel at one with everyone and everything as well as with the Divine Dreamer. When you open your heart, liberation from this dimension will get closer.*

Father paused and scanned the heavens. "Isn't it beautiful Narbiah?"

"The night sky littered with twinkling lights? Yes Father."

"Oh yes, that too, but I meant that the heart chakra in the body has exactly three chakras or rainbow colours below and three above. Let's continue."

Wedran, so creative and poetic, always noticed things unseen by others. I wanted to hug him.

*Blue – Speaking your truth brings your power and your potential together. With an open heart your focus will be on harmony, peace and gentleness and your words will reflect that. The colour blue is located at your throat energy center and your words create your reality. Know this well. Choose your words with care. Once they leave your lips and mind, they will go forth into the ether of the planet and create a reality that is congruent with your intention. Make your words - your intention - as loving and as kind as you can.*

*Indigo – This purple-blue of the forehead energy center, asks you to look beyond the veil of illusion and delusion. Nothing is as it seems and to hold dogmatic views on anything will cause a thickening of the energy that holds you to this dimension. Use the powerful insight and intuition that comes from an open heart, open mind and acceptance of the Divine Dream as all perfect, to step beyond the veil to freedom. Prison walls are of your own making and illusionary - set yourself free. Psychic powers will naturally occur at this stage, but do not give your self airs. At this point the ego will fight for its right to control you and will tempt you with delusions of grandeur. You are close to becoming a lucid dreamer in the Divine Dream. Be careful that you don't blow it now. There is only the purple to go.*

"Blow it? Do you mean their own pipe?" Father cackled at his own joke while I gave him a wry smile. We both instinctively looked up, checking the planetary bodies. Suddenly we stared at each other in the darkness, both sensing something but not sure what. An imperceptible hum hung behind the sound of night birds and rustling leaves that we felt rather than heard.

"What's happening Father, do you know?" I whispered.

"I most definitely *do* know. Prepare to bow my child." He stood tall and expectant. The accelerator felt like lead in my hand and if Wedran didn't seem so smilingly content, I'm sure I would have felt fear.

The etheric web of the planet began to wobble, like a vertical plate of jelly, and through it I could just make out the female figure of Racli, a High Elemental Princess. We had spoken on many occasions, but she was always in the Earth's dimension. The wobbling of the etheric web meant she was coming in from the outside. I was highly confused while my Father was apparently highly bemused. I slipped the Accelerator into my pocket.

Racli stepped through the web and as instructed I bowed my head in deference to this great being. For an Elemental she was remarkably tall, 6 foot or more and her huge slanted eyes were almost on the sides of her head like a cow's. She was hauntingly beautiful with long delicate fingers. I ached to be touched by her. Feelings such as these often overcame me when I was in the presence of Elementals. Wedran told me long ago that I'd had many incarnations in their world and I was the product of one of our soul family breeding with a water sprite. I had straddled both worlds for eons and it had been a great source of learning and understanding for me. But it also made it difficult to leave for the Omega dimension as I would be leaving some 'family' behind. Every plant, every stone, every bird and animal was connected to me, but I knew attachments would keep me stuck.

Racli's frond-like hands traced airy patterns as she spoke. Her voice was much rougher that you'd expect from someone from the fairy kingdoms, and commanded our attention.

"You did not think you could leave without my farewell surely?"

"Beloved Racli," I ventured, absolutely non-plussed at her entrance. "I'm having trouble with seeing you come from the outside into this dimension. I didn't know Elementals could ever leave the Earth."

"And I suppose you know everything Narbiah?" She lowered her voice and turned her head on an angle that I found a tad intimidating. Her power was unquestionable. Father was enjoying himself.

"Welcome Princess and we are indeed honoured that you find the time to farewell us." He bowed again.

"I was drawn by your message stick Narbiah. Anything that gets Hue Menn off the beloved Mother Earth quicker deserves recognition. It's a sad day when we have to seek forests elsewhere in the galaxies to live because of the greed on this planet."

"Is that where you have been Princess? Looking for new homes for my half brothers and sisters?" I asked her.

"Yes, sweet Narbiah, but so far I am the only one who has been able to make the transition from this dimension to another. I come to you in this moment with a request. Inter-breeding has worked between our energy systems once before, so I wish for you to carry in your belly an Elemental foetus that will disperse us through the galaxies as you travel between worlds." Racli made a flourish with the finger fronds, all the while gluing my eyes to her with her a powerful magnetism.

"Omigod! You want be to become pregnant to a plant?" I tried to lighten the atmosphere, but only my father snorted, before remembering who stood before us. I was ashamed of my quip then.

"Sorry Princess, no disrespect intended. I'm just having trouble accepting the idea of pregnancy and the whole idea of who the father would be and so on. Time is running out. The portal will have to be created in the next hour at the latest".

Racli glowered at me and hissed.

"The father of the foetus awaits my command. I await you quiescence!"

Wedran coughed and in that split second I read their thoughts. He told her he had given me the potion as promised.

"You promised what?" I yelled. "You knew about this, Father?" I felt betrayed somehow and started to walk in angry circles around Lymei's skull. The crystals caught the moonlight and created an eerie glow. The diamond between my Great Grandmother's teeth looked like she was smoking a cigarette. I started to rant and rave about being tricked by both my families when I went bang up against the most gorgeous, divine energy I've ever felt. My head jerked up and standing a few feet away was an Elemental, so handsome I caught my breath. I spun around to my father and Racli, but the space was empty. I was alone with this god. Alone and in love. He spoke and his voice melted my bones.

"I am Mornan, your Soul twin Narbiah, as unusual as that

might sound – an Elemental and a Hue Mann - but so be it. Our coming together is ordained by the Divine Dreamer. I love you so divinely, so completely; I love you as I love myself. I am and will be honoured to give you my seed."

Our energy fields vibrated with an intensity that bespoke our feelings as they merged together. It had been many lifetimes since I had experienced this intensity and I vaguely remembered my time with the Elementals as one of them. Our coming together was not purely physical; it was a merging of Souls. The cemetery danced with the colours of our rainbow, flashing through us and around us and lit up the portal that would soon transport Wedran and I to the Omega dimension. Mornan was the most exquisitely beautiful being I had ever lain with. The child that would come from this union would surely be a masterpiece of magic.

From a deep trance I heard my father's voice.

"Narbiah, Narbiah, the time is close now. Are you ready?"

I opened my eyes and saw Wedran and Racli smiling at me.

"Where is Mornan?" I whispered, but I already knew the answer. It would have been impossible for me to leave if he were here, so he had gone.

"Thank you dear Narbiah." The fronds stroked my face and I shuddered with delight. "But wait! We haven't finished reading your chronicles. Quickly let us finish, perhaps you might let me add something." Racli would have her way no matter what, but in that moment I would have given her my very life.

"You were up to the Purple Hue I believe."

Father grinned and nodded his lovely old head.

"Oh! You got the rest did you Princess?"

*Purple – Once you can see beyond the veil, you will be sorely tested in certain areas. Your intentions and aspirations will manifest like lightening, therefore you must make your every intention honourable and every aspiration holy. Your vibratory rate has increased enormously* since you first came to the Earth plane. Energy <u>will</u> manifest and slower energy manifests slowly. You will now manifest your intentions very fast, so no longer can you have a trivial, throwaway wish. It will happen. And fast. If you wish for an excuse to be able to shirk a responsibility, be prepared for something untoward to happen to you. Those thoughts alone will slow down your energy vibration. You must maintain dignity, not from a blown up sense of self-importance, but a dignity born of integrity that is unshakeable. Rather than self-importance you will walk with such self-esteem that anything anyone does or does not do will concern you – you will only seek to be one with the Divine Dreamer. Then you will be aware of a lightening of the purple to violet as white light begins to pervade your dreaming. The white is a mixing of all the rainbow colours and is proof that you have integrated them all into your energy field. The Earth dimension is the only place where white is seen in an aura. If you see golden-white light then you will know it is of a higher dimension and you are ready to leave.

May the Divine Dream fulfill itself blissfully in you. Farewell."

I was relieved that the scanning of my chronicles was over. Racli looked thoughtful and brushed her beautiful forehead with those frond-like fingers. Wedran said that we must now bury the message stick under Lymei's skull and complete the portal with the Accelerator.

"But dear Friends you forget to ask me if there is something of import to add to the chronicles." Racli deftly snatched the message stick from my father's hand, placed in on the ground and stepped on it. Elemental's inner vision was not in the forehead as it is in Hue Menn, but in their feet.

"Trust me, while I record on the message stick, I will speak aloud my information for Hue Menn, so you will know exactly what I share." Racli centered herself, while father and I searched the sky for the planetary configuration that we needed to leave. Wedran shrugged his shoulders at the urgency in my eyes when I looked at him. Racli began her monologue while I twitched nervously, because the Accelerator was now getting hot in my pocket.

"*Greetings Hue Menn, this is Racli, High Princess of the Otherworld of Elemental Energies. Please heed my words. It is true what my friend Narbiah has told you of the rainbow colours and the hues, but you must know more if you are truly to save the Earth from total annihilation. As the intellect of Hue Menn became more and more dominant, your intuition diminished and the exploitation of this planet Earth was rationalized and deemed necessary. Narbiah has explained the energy centers in your body. Now I ask that when you have completed the transcendence and can see gold in the aura, this is to be your next step.*

Racli paused and challenged us with the look of royalty. Despite our sense of urgency, we were vitally interested and nodded simultaneously. Father's old hand slipped reassuringly around mine. The Accelerator began to burn and I could see a faint golden glow through my robe where it lay in my pocket.

"*You must now allow the colours of the Earth to be returned to the Great Mother for healing. Allow the red, orange, yellow and green to flow down and out of your energy system into the beloved mother Earth. Immediately you do this willingly and with an open heart - not your intellect - the higher colours will flow down and fill your energy centers with a different vibration. Blue will then be the colour of the base chakra, indigo will center itself in the sex chakra, and violet will fill the solar plexus. Automatically you will be gifted with a new patterning. Diamond or crystal will be placed in the heart center, silver will fill your throat chakra, gold will be the colour of the third eye in the forehead and the colour of magenta will resonate from your crown. This is called the very soul of GOD, the Great Omnipotent Dreamer. Why do this? Hue Menn will need to be prepared for the next dimension before they leave, otherwise they will feel uncomfortable in the new vibration. High Priest Wedran and his daughter Narbiah will leave with an energy system modified for the Omega Dimension. As will you, when your time comes.*

*I, Princess Racli of the Otherworld, ask that you see this modification of your energy system as a matter of urgency. Farewell.*"

Racli handed the message stick to me and without a word sat with an attitude of spectator on a low branch of an old Ginkgo tree nearby. Father took his cue and motioned me to join him in the portal. I placed the Accelerator under the chin of the skull. It was hot and glowed with an eerie pale moonlight colour. The charge it created activated the nails around the circle and they also began to glow. Small lightening bolts leapt from the Accelerator to the nails, around and around the circle. Then the crystals in Lymei's skull began to glow – all the colours of the rainbow arcing from the skull to the nails to the Accelerator. It was so beautiful I was entranced. My eyes searched my Father's face for a sign of fear in leaving Earth, but he was as ecstatic as I and I grinned so wide that he laughed out loud. Then it happened! The etheric web of the planet was sucked into a vortex over the portal we'd created. Wedran took my arm and together we stepped into the spiraling vortex. We looked up as one and saw that the vortex was part of an unending tunnel – a wormhole that had branches at intervals along it.

"Did you know about the new colours in the chakras Narbiah?" Wedran raised his eyebrow and the tattoo contorted. I answered truthfully.

"No! What about you?" I said starting to feel disoriented as if every cell in my body was slowly disintegrating. My father held my arm tighter.

"Would I sound arrogant if I said yes? Seeing golden-white light in our auras is always the signal. You as part Elemental would have willingly surrendered the red, orange, yellow and green from yourself ages ago."

We started to get a transparency to our forms, but he saw my head nod. I was past physically speaking and projected my question to his inner being.

"Father, do you know the energetic blueprint of the new colours?"

Before he could answer in any way, we were whisked upward so fast it was uncanny, because we felt no movement at all, but streaked through the tunnels faster than light beams. The silence was unimaginable and the tunnels went off to left and right and we changed direction many times. Then we knew we were slowing down by the fact that the walls of the tunnels were more in focus. They appeared to have no physical substance, just walls of creamy-greyish light that got denser and denser as we slowed. Up ahead of us we saw the image of Great, Great Grandmother Lymei and a whole band of soul family. Father and I gave each other the thumbs up. We had made the transition and we couldn't wait to experience life in the Omega Dimension.

Lymei raised her hand in greeting which incongruously looked like a policemen stopping the traffic. Behind the group, the tunnel came to an abrupt end. Beyond was black sky dotted with stars. Lymei spoke then.

"Beloved Ones, we are now all assembled ready for the next stage of the Dream. The Omega Dimension awaits us. Soon our souls will join again as The One and our combined vibration will easily make the shift possible. Our time as Hue Menn is no more."

This was an unparalleled adventure. Thankfully Lymei had traveled ahead and could conduct us through. Father stuck his elbow into my ribs to get my attention and then bowed his old head.

"Goodbye my sweet child. Who knows in what forms we will meet again."

Then all one hundred and forty four thousand of us stepped into the void of space.

to be continued...or not

*Some people believe that family hold the key to their security;*

*but perhaps it is a silent longing for the Soul-Family that makes them weep.*

*And what is security? Do we really need it?*

*Spiritual Masters have never worried over such stuff and have set themselves free from family entanglements and expectations.*
*So I wondered how it would be to just have oneself?*
*To be so emptied of expectation and desire that we simply 'be'. Not wanting this or that.*
*Just being present*
*to the essence of who we really are.*

*The train ride of your life could be the catalyst for such an experience...*

GM

# TRAIN RIDE TO NANPULGUDJURI

Calcutta was an unrelenting rowdy sideshow; incessant car horns, voices over loud speakers and people jostling. Felicity arrived in the middle of a stifling-hot night, so jet-lagged that the stench of the place was not as ghastly as she expected. The beggars were much more so. Filthy, haunted looking creatures that stretched blackened fingers toward her, with eyes even blacker that seemed to claw at her soul. The paleness of Felicity's skin had the air of a spectre amid the darkness on the streets and she felt very insecure.

"I must do this," Felicity told herself and strode toward the waiting car. Some parents in India are known to cut off their children's legs or arms or mutilate them in other ways to illicit sympathy. A beggar stepped from a blackened doorway to block her path. He only had one eye, which he now fixed on her terrified face. Felicity recoiled as he lurched on broken sticks toward her.

"*Rupee*"? *Rupee*?" the legless one begged.

The hotel driver took her arm and chided her for even thinking that she might hand over some cash. "It encourages them madam. It is better that we do not encourage them."

All night long the beggar's single tragic eye was burned on Felicity's heart like a cattle brand and she wondered what the next day's train journey would bring.

She had booked a first class sleeping car, which turned out to be third world by Western standards. The toilets were a squat-hole in the floor and the garbage bin was an 'open the door and throw it out' affair. Felicity thought the entire country must be one big rubbish heap. The train had no private compartments, foreigners and locals all bunking together, side by side, upper and lower, with wandering passengers and hawkers traipsing up and down the narrow corridor between bunks calling, "Coffee, chai?" Felicity smiled at anyone who looked at her, hoping for a conversation in English. She desperately wanted to know what the protocol for such a trip was, but no one seemed interested in talking to her. A constant buzz of Hindi, the clacking of train wheels and the occasional shout from somewhere along the train, made her feel very alone. She made her way, lurching with the train, to the toilet. With bracing legs she stared at the hole in the floor and took in the room. The cubicle was much larger than a standard toilet. Through the hole, which was flanged by a stainless steel collar, Felicity stared wide-eyed at the track moving as a conveyor belt beneath her. A plastic jug hung from a rope, swinging like a pole dancer in unison with the rocking train. A filthy basin was clamped onto a perishing pipe on one wall. It was a balancing act to relieve her exploding bladder, while straddling the hole, holding her skirt high enough not to get wet with one hand

and holding the rim of metal with the other. She wondered how fat, elderly or sick people managed such contortions. The jug was obviously used to flush anything one left behind. She shuddered when she thought that children of beggars might scavenge on the railway tracks, which, like a ten thousand mile open sewer, ran the length of India. Felicity stared incredulously as a dead rat, amid rotting garbage flashed under the train. She concluded that the hole in the floor was dangerously large.

The guard delivered a blanket, two sheets and a small pillow to each passenger for them to make their own bed. The bunks were hard vinyl and absurdly narrow. The locals immediately commandeered the lower beds, leaving Felicity to hoist her self to the remaining bunk, clutching her bag as if it were a baby. The bed made, she drew the curtain that separated her from the other passengers, whom had done the same. A protruding arm swung loosely across from her cubbyhole, the occupant already snoring. High emotion had exhausted her and she slept like a corpse to the rocking of the train.

Loud voices woke her. The rise and fall of Hindi, some European, perhaps German and very distant English punctuated with sharp intakes of breath. Through a gap in the window curtain, the fields outside had the ethereal quality of pre-dawn. Porters and guards ran along the cramped corridors, yelling to each other, creating dramatic effect and preventing Felicity from more deep sleep. Fitfully dosing, she eventually sat in her bed and cleansed her face, brushed her hair into a neat ponytail and applied a makeup. She ate the nuts and fruit she had brought, then opening the curtain, slithered down to clean her teeth with her bottled water in the toilet. A tired-looking woman in a sari, holding a filthy mop waved Felicity away.

"I am sorry Madam, we are cleaning this toilet. Please go to the other end."

"Oh! You speak very good English," said Felicity delighted. "Do you know how much longer before Nanpulgudjuri?"

"We very much apologise for the delay Madam, but you see a

girl had a baby here last night." The woman gestured toward the gaping hole in the floor.

"Not here, not …?" Felicity was aghast.

"Yes Madam. Poor baby slipped through onto the tracks. That is why the train stopped last night."

Suddenly wanting to vomit, Felicity mouthed soundless words, "Oh God no!" and found her tormented way back to her seat.

"What bloody awful place *is* this?" She sniffed up the tears dripping off her nostrils.

Three years before Felicity had sat shocked and breaking beside her own premature baby, as his tiny body lay in a humid crib that tried to keep him alive and failed. From her bag she took her journal and opened it to the poem she had written then.

> *MY BABY MARCUS*
> *More insistent than water drops on tin.*
> *I want to smash that clock*
> *but every tic is a second of his life.*
>
> *His body a gestation mistake*
> *like a baby kangaroo*
> *who's in a pouch of glass.*
>
> *What chance to grow into a big Red*
> *that stamps his foot*
> *to echo on the earth?*
>
> *He grimaces. Matchstick fingers unfurl*
> *then re-curl.*
> *Is it pain my Treasure? Or do you dream*
>
> *Of ticking*
> *louder than your mother's heartbeat;*

*calling up your last breath.*

Forced back into her grief, she remembered how ultimately her baby died, along with her marriage. Post-traumatic stress clawed through painful memories and replayed their last conversation.

"Where are you going Mark? *Why* are you going? I don't know you anymore!" Felicity had cried splintering - disintegrating.

"Since baby Marcus died I don't know *myself* Felly. I'm numb. I can't seem to love anymore. Think I'll go to India – they need engineers for the Border Roads Org. Take care of yourself."

Now Felicity was going to find Mark. She had no way of knowing that she would find much more instead.

\*\*\*

The train heaved into Nanpulgudjeri at 10.12am. Extra had been paid so that Felicity could have the 4WD taxi to herself. Her driver, Ashwani, was from Sikkim and spent much of his time as a Sherpa in Nepal. He spoke good English but they each kept to their own thoughts most of the time. The road winding up into the Himalayas was frighteningly narrow, terrifyingly steep and seriously damaged in places. Hundreds of cars and trucks, like a speeding ant trail, negotiated passing; sometimes with only three wheels on the road - the other wheel hanging precariously over the thousand metre drop to the Teesta River below. Signs posted by the Border Roads Org. were like comic relief. 'Whisky Is Risky' and 'Be Gentle With My Curves' might have had Felicity laughing in another lifetime.

"Something's wrong with engine Madam," frowned Ashwani, white teeth flashing in his brown handsome face. "Get fixed at next village. We OK. No problem."

The village was one building, hanging off a high cliff like a boulder ready to fall. Here was the doctor, mechanic, shopkeeper, husband, father and friend – all in one smiling old man, who said the engine could be fixed in a few days.

"No problem M'am. We happy if you stay here." His wife and children were all nodding and

smiling in delight.

Felicity, usually fearful of the unknown, curiously felt safe, as she dropped onto the little corner mattress in a room she would share with seven children. The warm and friendly family adopted Felicity as their own and she thought it surreal to be staying in the Himalayas with complete strangers, as she drifted into a dreamless sleep.

Before dawn she had an impulse to walk. Slipping silently from the house, following the road, she fully feasted on the spectacular views. A rooster crowed in the mist and Felicity sighed; relaxed for the first time in years.

"Good morning." The whisper on the still air stroked her ears. She spun around scanning the area. A beggar, or so she thought, stood with his back to her, facing the deep valley below.

"Welcome," he said with a trace of authority.

Felicity said 'thank you' and stopped beside him. She was afraid to look at him, memories of mutilated faces alive in her mind.

"Why are you here, my child?" He turned dark and mysterious eyes toward her. This man was no beggar. Suddenly, despite her natural reserve, Felicity began her story of loss, babbling details of her marriage and baby, wondering all the while who the compelling stranger was.

"I'm Felicity." She extended a hand, which he held in both of his dark brown ones.

"Oh *I* know who you are. It is *you* who do not know who *you* are - yet. I am called Yogeshwar Muni by some." Only a glimmer of a smile danced across his ageless face. "Be well. Hari Om." He crossed the road and was lost in the forest before she could answer.

That night she dreamt of a beckoning guru in a cave and found herself telling Ashwani of her encounter with the stranger the next morning.

"Yes Madam, if one's car breaks down here, you are expected."

"Expected?"

"Oh yes, when the student is ready, the teacher appears. When the teacher is ready, the student is summoned." Ashwani was serious.

"Have you ever met him Ashwani?" Felicity was more than curious now.

"No Miss Felicity. The Master never leaves his cave."

"But... but I met him yesterday. At dawn on the road!" Felicity pointed toward the cliff edge.

"The Master appears sometimes, but his body is always in his cave." Ashwani was very matter-of-fact.

That night the full moon was hidden by the endless cloud that clothes the Himalayas. Felicity couldn't sleep. The guru's eyes looked at her behind her closed lids. With blanket-wrapped body, she tiptoed past the sleeping family and walked again up the quiet, dark road as clouds parted occasionally to flash moonlight across the peaks. Entranced by the surreal spectacle, Felicity sat cross-legged on the spot where she had her first encounter with the 'teacher'.

"Thank you for coming." His voice, with the same musical quality, made her jump. Felicity smiled self-consciously and with hands in prayer at her heart, she bowed her head, acknowledging Yogeshwar. He silently sat beside her, wrapped also in a blanket.

"Let us meditate together." He settled himself and rhythmically and sweetly began to chant, *"Om Namah Shivaya."* Soon Felicity drifted into a very quiet internal space. Dreamlike, she saw herself again, in her mind's eye, standing at the entrance to a cave and Yogeshwar beckoning her to enter.

"Enter child," he said. "I have a story for you."

Smiling kind eyes toward her, he began.

"Once there was a great Master who was walking about India with his chosen disciple. They stopped under the shade of a tree.

"Please go down to that river and get me some water," the Master told the young man. So he did - but as he squatted to fill the jug, he looked up to see a lovely young woman walking toward him. Well, it was love at first sight for them both, and she invited him to come to her village to meet her parents. So he did – his master forgotten completely! Her family loved him and invited him to stay. So he did – and after many weeks he was so besotted with the girl, he asked her father for her hand in marriage. The entire village celebrated the wedding and then the young man set about building a house for his wife. Master completely forgotten! Soon the couple had a child, then another and another and another. The site of their home was on a hill overlooking the river. One year the monsoons were so strong, that the river flooded and came into their house! The water kept on rising and rising, flooding the first floor and the second floor, so the young man moved his family to the roof...but still the water rose. During the night one by one his children and his wife were swept into the swirling floodwaters and drowned. The young man spent the entire night swimming, calling to them, searching for them, almost drowning himself. By morning the storms had passed. Exhausted and almost unconscious he found himself on the banks of the swollen river. He lay shocked and uncomprehending of the night's events, and then on the clear morning air, he heard his guru's voice.

"Where are you my boy, I've been waiting nearly an hour for my water?"

***

Birdcalls percolated through the dawn. Felicity felt a tug on her blanket and opened her eyes. A small monkey was making snatching movements with tiny black hands while baring his teeth at her, trying to look fierce. Felicity held its eyes with her own calm ones, and it moved away without a quarrel. Her legs were numb when she tried to move.

"I've been here for hours," she thought while wiggling her legs in the air, stretching out the constricted blood vessels. "What an extraordinary country this is," she concluded, and began a reflection of the night's events.

She reached into her bag for her journal and began poetically recording the teachings of Yogeshwar as though he was the writer.

## GRACE OF THE GURU

*Like mist shrouding Katjanjunga –*
*blending of perpetual cloud with spirit rising*
*from the body of the rivers*
*She comes and goes.*
*The word 'felicity' means bliss.*
*She didn't know.*
*The mind is a conjuring trickster.*

Loss? *She pleads.*
   *Is illusionary.*
   *Black hole created by that trickster.*

Emptiness then?
   *Subjective. Space to choose.*
Choice?
   *Seduction or freedom?*
   *You choose. Are the mystic Himalayas empty because there are no*
*Hungry Jacks?*
*Yet hungry Jack and Jill's do come - clawing through the grey shards of*
*glacial river beds to find gold.*
Gold?
   *The door to Shambala is not in the mud.*
*It shimmers on the ether higher than thoughts fly.*

We? Humans?
   *People are asleep. They dream and think it real.*
Bodies are real though?

*Or entrapment - bondage and limitation.*

What of needs?
*Just the caterwauling ego, "I want! I want!"*
*Squawking like a baby bird.*

And feelings?
*Merely temporal. Strangely forming then disappearing as the*
*mountain mist.*

And romance?
*Chemical concoction in a brain.*
*Never lasting bliss.*

Freedom then?
*Not judging. Experience <u>is</u> the meaning.*

Then? The past?
*Distorted memories and never truth.*

So now?
*Space between breaths.*
*Pregnant point of time between memory and dream.*
*Now is the crest of a wave? The edge where change is conceived?*

And life then?
*The catalyst for transformation.*
*Just breathe and be.*
*Felicity means bliss.*

I didn't know.

\*\*\*

"Good morning Miss Felicity! I trust you had a good night?"
Ashwani, who had slept in his vehicle, was cleaning his teeth by

the roadside as she appeared. "Good news! Engine part comes this morning. We leave soon - be at Gangtok today. I hope your appointment with Border Roads Organisation is not made difficult by the delay?"

She threw back her head and laughed out loud something she had not done for years.

"Ashwani, would it be alright if you took me back to Nanpulgudjeri instead? I'm going home.

"Where is home Miss Felicity?"

She closed her eyes and sighed.

"Home is the part of my breath that neither hungers after the inhalation or longs for the exhalation. Home lingers in my footprints like the fragrance of frangipanis and slips soft fingers into my hand as we walk. Looking for my home was futile because home just is and like the storyteller it sits at the hearth waiting for the wide-eyed child to sit at its feet. So I came and sat and he read. His words spoke of a lost soul who wasn't lost after all."

Ashwani, deeply moved, grinned like a proud parent.

"Nanpulgudguri here we come!"

---

*The end? Of course not.*
*Life and death, loving and losing continue.*
*For every feather that falls from a*
*bird, there is a story to be told.*
*And I continue to wonder...*

*Grandmother Moon*

Printed in the United States
By Bookmasters